Mystery

Bill couldn't wait to tell Cynthia. "Someone named Charlotte Wodehouse turned in a poem to the literary magazine that is just fantastic. I was so blown away by it that I've been carrying it around in my notebook. I couldn't wait to show it to you."

Cynthia studied his face, she hoped casually. He didn't seem to be playing a game with her. "Charlotte Wodehouse?" she said. "I don't know her."

"I'd be surprised if you did. There's nobody by that name in the student handbook, and it's obviously a pen name. I wish I could find out who she is. There was something about her poem that fascinated me. This may sound corny, but I feel like I have a kind of bond with her."

Cynthia felt as if a hippopotamus had just sat on her stomach. She thought her heart would burst. He was beginning to be aware of the special feeling between them, too! Of course he didn't know that she was Charlotte Wodehouse, but her poem had touched him just the way — no, far more than — she had hoped it would.

"Bill — " she began, then closed her mouth. How could she confess to him now?

**Books from Scholastic
in the Couples series:**

SECRETS

COUPLES

SECRETS

M. E. Cooper

SCHOLASTIC INC.
New York Toronto London Auckland Sydney

ISBN 0–590–40160–2

Copyright © 1986 by Cloverdale Press. All rights reserved. Published by Scholastic Inc.

12 11 10 9 8 7 6 5 4 3 2 1   3   6 7 8 9/8 0 1/9

Printed in the U.S.A.   06

SECRETS

Chapter
1

Bill Magnuson gave a shout of laughter. "Unbelievable!" he snorted.

Cynthia Walker looked up from her biology homework and brushed her fluffy brown hair away from her face. She had dropped by the *Imagination* office for a few minutes after school, planning to walk home with Bill, and was still there an hour later keeping busy while he read the latest submissions. As associate editor of the Kennedy High School literary magazine, he took his work very seriously; he also got a lot of fun out of it.

"Unbelievable!" he repeated.

"What is?"

"This poem! Listen: 'The moon was a ghostly galleon floating on storm-tossed seas. . . .' What do you think of that?" Bill grinned mischievously.

Cynthia narrowed her eyes, wrinkled her nose, and thought very hard. Above all she wanted to

1

avoid saying anything Bill would think was dumb. "I don't know," she began. "I guess I like it. It's really . . . vivid."

He snorted again. "Yeah, I think so, too."

"Then why — " Cynthia stopped in confusion.

"I thought so the first time I read it, too. When was that, back in eighth grade? *You* remember, Cyn: 'The highwayman came riding, riding, riding, riding. . . .' It looks like this freshperson, whose name I won't mention, liked the poem so much that she couldn't resist swiping the best parts for herself." He scrawled a brief note on the bottom of the page. "There," he added, "I don't think she'll make that mistake again!"

Cynthia giggled. She knew how funny and biting Bill's literary criticism could be. It wasn't hard to imagine how the unknown student would feel when she read his comment. Cynthia felt her own cheeks grow warm with sympathetic embarrassment even as she enjoyed the humorous side of the situation. After all, it could happen to anyone. Being a writer herself, she knew what it meant to be influenced by a well-loved poem or story.

Bill fished something else out of the submission box, glanced at it, and groaned. "A book report on *Silas Marner*. Just what I needed to make my day! Come on, let's get out of here. I don't think I can face any more."

Bill lived only three houses away from Cynthia. They first got to know each other the day she fell out of a tree in fifth grade, landed on him, and broke his arm. In the six years since, they'd become close friends. Hardly a day went by that they didn't spend some time together. Cynthia knew Bill so well that she took him for granted. He was simply part of her life, like the oak tree in her front yard or the kitchen stove. She never even saw him anymore, not really . . . until a few weeks ago.

Suddenly she'd found herself looking at him as if he were a guy she had just met. Her jaw had practically hit the floor — she felt as if she was still blinking from the vision. Now, as they walked home through the quiet streets of Rose Hill, she stole glances at him out of the corner of her eye. The boy walking next to her was tall and slender, with a thin, clever face, sandy blond hair that stood up or flopped down just as it chose, and pale blue eyes that twinkled at unexpected moments. He was that and so much more. He could tuck one leg behind his head; he had wonderfully strong forearms, thanks to his passion for golf; he was as gentle as a lamb when it came to taking care of his little brother Kenny, he. . . .

"Two cents," Bill said suddenly, as they turned onto their block. This was a private joke; Bill had once said that they both had such fantastic thoughts that they were worth twice as much as most people's.

Cynthia blinked. Caught in the act. The most difficult thing for her to keep in mind was that while her eyes had been opened to Bill, his hadn't opened to her. She was still his old pal, Cynthia.

"N — nothing," she stammered, improvising. "Uh, I was wondering how long it'll be before it's

3

warm enough for the beach. I miss the ocean, don't you?"

"Um-hum." He smiled. "Remember that time our folks rented that awful shack near Newport Beach together? And we ended up having to sleep on the living room floor?"

"What do you mean, sleep?" Cynthia said indignantly. "You kept telling one ghost story after another, and every time you finished one, the house started creaking. The only thing missing was the creepy music! I spent the whole night zipped inside my sleeping bag for safety, thanks to you!"

Bill laughed. "You were a lot easier to scare back then. That reminds me: The Film Club is showing what's supposed to be one of the ten corniest horror flicks ever made, tomorrow after school. Think you might be interested?"

"Sure," Cynthia said, after a pause. "It sounds like fun."

"Yeah. I think I'll go, too. Maybe I'll see you there."

They had just reached the Walkers' driveway. Cynthia turned to Bill. "Should I save you a seat?" she asked casually. She hoped her face didn't reveal too much.

"Don't bother," he replied with a smile and a shrug. "I'm not sure if I can make it. There's a lot of work I ought to do for the magazine. I can always get a play-by-play from you."

"Sure," Cynthia said, trying to keep the disappointment out of her voice. "See you," she added as she started for the house, giving a wave back

4

over her shoulder. Bill stood at the foot of her driveway until she reached the door, as he always did.

"Yeah, bye," he called. "And oh, Cyn? Don't forget to check in the closet and under the bed before you go to sleep. Newport Beach isn't the only place that has monsters, you know!"

As usual at this time of day, the Walker house was empty. The only sounds were the hum of the refrigerator and the ticking of the antique clock on the mantel. Cynthia's dad worked at the Library of Congress, in downtown Washington, and rarely got home before six. Her mom, a popular and busy pediatrician, had office hours two evenings a week, on top of her daytime hours and hospital rounds. Cynthia admired her parents and respected their careers, but she couldn't help wishing they spent more time at home, like some of her classmates' parents.

Cynthia made a beeline through the house to the kitchen. Dropping her book bag on the table, she opened the fridge and seriously contemplated its contents. Today nothing really tempted her. She grabbed an apple and went upstairs to her room.

Like the rest of the house, Cynthia's room was furnished in a functional modern style. Her clothes hid in white stackable drawer units. Her single bed, also white, concealed a trundle bed within it, for when friends slept over. In the daytime a bunch of cushions helped it pretend to be a couch. The white shelves attached to the far wall held books, half a dozen Steiff animals, and other childhood treasures. Her desk was a simple slab of plastic-covered wood, resting on two white metal file cabinets.

The object that brought the room to life was a poster she had found in Georgetown, a full-color photograph of a museum in Paris called the Beaubourg. The fanciful building, with its brightly painted pipes and girders running every which way, strongly appealed to Cynthia's imagination. Someday she'd like to go there and explore the whole place, inside and out.

In the meantime, she could get started on her homework. She didn't have a lot, and since she was an efficient worker she could easily be finished in time to get dinner started, and have the evening free. But instead of opening her notebook and making another stab at her biology assignment, Cynthia found herself gazing out the window, chin in hand, daydreaming. Daydreaming about Bill.

His eyes. His hair. His stupidity! Cynthia's smile changed to a frown. After all, *he* had asked *her* if she wanted to go to the movie. Any other guy would have realized that it sounded as if he was asking her to go with him. But not best friend Bill.

Cynthia admitted to herself that she didn't really care one way or the other about the movie. But if Bill was going to be there, she wanted to be there, too. She knew they'd have a great time chuckling and groaning in unison, then stop at the sub shop afterward and rehash the entire film.

They'd have fun because they always had fun together.

She enjoyed spending time with him. She could come right out and tell him that! Cynthia's big green eyes grew even bigger at the thought, and her stomach felt as though she'd just stepped off the high dive. After all, she and Bill weren't in grammar school anymore; good friends should be able to talk about their feelings for one another. But that was just it. Her feelings were deeper than those of a good friend now. Bill was comfortable with her, as she was with him; they were pals. But if he sensed that she wanted something more from him, he might stop being comfortable. He might begin to avoid her. She could ruin any chance for a romance with him, and spoil their very special friendship in the process.

Cynthia sighed. She couldn't risk it. Bill was her closest friend, and losing him was the worst thing she could imagine. If keeping Bill's friendship meant hiding her deeper feelings for him, then hide them she would. It made her sad to think she couldn't share this new joy, but at least she would still have her old friend. That was something, and a lot better than nothing.

Cynthia shook her head to chase these disappointing thoughts away. If all she could do was hope Bill would someday return her feelings, then she'd hope hard.

Cynthia glanced at her pile of school books, but thought better of it. Instead she decided to put her introspective mood to work by writing in her diary. The diary was one of the few secrets she

7

kept from both her family and from Bill. She took it now from a locked drawer in her desk.

The book was as big as a loose-leaf notebook, clothbound, with a delicate pattern of flowers and leaves. The pages were smooth, thick, and cream-colored. Cynthia ran her hand lightly over the cover, then opened the book to the middle. She glanced at the words at the top of the page:

The night is wise to shroud itself in darkness. . . .

Nodding, she turned to the next page and smiled.

My neighbor's puppy bites its tail
And runs in circles endlessly. . . .

The following page was blank. Cynthia reached for a pen. This was the secret of the diary: She was a poet.

She had started writing poems almost by accident, after her thirteenth birthday. An aunt in Chicago had sent her a beautiful little diary, complete with lock and key, and a note saying that every teenage girl ought to keep one. Cynthia's first entry was an account of her birthday, including a complete list of presents, followed by her thoughts about leaving childhood and entering a new stage of her life.

She soon discovered that she wasn't a natural diary keeper. Half the time she forgot to write anything, then tried to catch up by pretending it was still two or three days earlier. She became bored with simply recording the events of her daily life. Who sat at the same table with her at lunch and who said what, funny or dumb comments made in class by teachers and students, what she wore,

8

what she had for dinner — before long her entries started to read like telegrams, until she stopped writing in the diary altogether.

The turning point came one warm spring evening. The azaleas were in blossom and the moon was just past full. Thirteen-year-old Cynthia sat in the backyard, her head tipped to look at the clear sky, wriggling her bare toes in the cool grass. There was something here she wanted to capture, and when she went inside, she opened her diary to record it all. After three or four sentences, however, she realized that her words were so flat and ordinary that they made the experience seem flat and ordinary, too.

Closing her eyes, she tried to recapture her magical mood, and from somewhere, an image came to her, of the world as a huge, purring cat. She picked up her pencil and wrote: "The moon is a saucer of buttermilk, lapped by the April breeze." She liked that, but she liked it even better when she broke it into two lines. Before she went to sleep that night, she had written her first poem.

She was very proud of her work, but shy about it, too. Her poem was something personal and private. It might seem merely silly to another person. Not only that, but her poem might not even be any good. *She* liked it, but what did she know? She couldn't bear to find out that what she thought was precious was really worthless.

Since that time Cynthia had always kept her poems and other scribblings carefully hidden. When she locked her diary back up this afternoon, she wished she could lock away her unsettling emotions about Bill as well. But it looked like they were staying with her. Cynthia smiled to herself. She couldn't help feeling positive about what life had in store for her in the immediate future. She opened up her biology book, figuring she could study and dream about Bill at the same time.

Chapter 2

The closer she got to the sub shop, the slower Phoebe Hall's footsteps became. Two stores away, she came to a complete stop. She looked around at the blue sky dotted with fluffy white clouds and felt the breeze stirring in her thick mane of red hair. Wasn't it much too nice a day to be indoors? The sub shop was bound to be crowded and noisy, and full of smoke, and she certainly — she prodded her tummy — didn't need anything heavy to eat. Why not pop into the grocery store, buy an apple, and take it to the park?

The plan tempted her, but she shook her head sternly. She knew the real reason she was reluctant to go in. It was the reason for most of the things she did and thought and felt these days: Griffin Neill. He was more constantly in her mind now than he had been before their relationship came to such an abrupt and shattering end.

Had it really been so short a time since he had told her that he was leaving New York and coming back to Rose Hill to be near her? She had been so happy to be with him again, and so proud when he won the role of Tony in a regional production of *West Side Story*. And when he asked her to come to a rehearsal, she had hardly anticipated that he was taking that opportunity to communicate to her that he was in love with another girl.

The moment she saw him singing "Somewhere" with his co-star Sarah Carter, Phoebe knew the truth. She tried to tell herself that he was simply a wonderful actor, but she knew better. She recognized the passion in his eyes. Once upon a time he had looked at her that way. When she confronted him about Sarah, Griffin didn't even attempt to deny or explain the change in his feelings.

Phoebe pulled her favorite Cub Scout shirt a little tighter around her. It was becoming a bit ragged from constant wear, but with it on she felt secure, more like her old self. Most of her friends were probably in the sub shop right now, bunched around one of the long picnic tables, talking and laughing and enjoying themselves. She couldn't mourn Griffin forever. It was sometimes lonely being "single" again, especially when there were so many happy couples in her crowd, but she could handle it.

Besides, her good friends Chris, Woody, Sasha, and the others had nothing but affection for her, and sympathy for her situation. When she was around them she could relax and be herself, whether or not she was still going with Griffin. They understood, and were with her one hundred percent. Then why was she still standing outside the sub shop acting as though somebody had glued her Reeboks to the pavement?

Phoebe might have spent another five or ten minutes engaged in internal debate except for the arrival of Kim Barrie, who came up behind her and grabbed her, making her shriek. Kim had moved to Rose Hill from Pittsburgh that winter, but with her bright smile and love for organizing things she'd already made a splash at Kennedy High. She'd made a splash with Phoebe's old friend Woody Webster, too; they'd become a steady couple.

"Hi," Kim said, still laughing at Phoebe's surprise. "Are you going to the sub shop?"

"I guess so," Phoebe said, with a rueful smile. "You, too, huh?"

Kim shook her head. "I'm on my way to make a delivery for Earthly Delights." Earthly Delights was the catering business Kim's mom had organized with her help. "Twelve dozen assorted tiny tea sandwiches, if you can believe it. My personal favorite is the egg and anchovy."

"Sounds like a pizza. They're serving those at the sub shop now? The place is getting pretty fancy!"

"No way." Kim laughed. "I'm taking them over to President Street, to a lady who's some sort of Washington lobbyist. She's having three dozen people to tea this afternoon. Let's see: That works

13

out to four sandwiches apiece, doesn't it? She must have hungry friends."

"Four *tiny* sandwiches," Phoebe said.

"Right; four tiny sandwiches apiece. She must have *small* hungry friends. Hey, would you do something? I told Woody I'd meet him here, before I knew about this delivery. Would you tell him about the tiny tea sandwiches, and that I'll call him this evening? I've really got to run."

"Sure," Phoebe said. She was glad of Kim's request; it was just the kick in the pants she needed.

She waved to Kim, then opened the thick wooden door of the sub shop. The place was just as crowded and noisy as she had expected. She stepped inside and glanced around, nodding and smiling at a few familiar faces. She wasn't distracted by the old motorcycle hanging on the wall, the dozens of Kennedy High pennants, or the stuffed bear in the far corner — they were just part of the familiar environment. Instead she focused on Woody, who was gesturing to her from where he stood at the counter.

She edged past a gaggle of sophomores and joined him. "Hey, Pheeb-a-rebop," Woody said, tucking his thumbs into the red suspenders that were his trademark, "I was wondering if you'd turn up. You're just in time to go halvesies on a large order of fries."

"Not me," she laughed. She ordered a diet soda and gave Woody Kim's message. "I guess Kim puts in a lot of time on her mom's business," she added, in a questioning tone.

"Um-hum," he said cheerfully. "It's great to

see her at work — she's so good at it! I've been helping out a little, too, mostly doing prep."

Phoebe giggled. "Do you have to wear an alligator shirt and Top Siders without socks?"

Woody laughed and poked her in the ribs. "Not that kind of prep, goofus! It means stuff like peeling potatoes and slicing cucumbers. Mrs. Barrie's promised to teach me how to make radish flowers next week. That's a real step up."

"Wow, next thing we know you'll be graduating to broccoli bouquets!"

"I'm not going to talk to you anymore," he huffed. "Some things are too important to be joked about . . . things like food! Oh, good, here comes our fries. Go grab a table, I'll bring them over."

"I'm not — " she began, then stopped. There wasn't much use in pretending she wouldn't end up eating half of Woody's order!

The table her crowd usually occupied was nearly full. At one end, Sasha Jenkins was sipping a cup of pink-colored herb tea and frowning at some scribbles on her yellow legal pad. Sasha was the editor of *The Red and the Gold*, the school newspaper. Next to her, Peter Lacey, WKND's star disk jockey, was telling a story to Janie Barstow. His handsome face was animated. Janie was quite a story herself; in a few short months she'd changed from a shy and gawky girl to the prom queen of Kennedy High. Her boyfriend, Henry Braverman, was probably at home working on the clothing designs that had made him one of the best-known students in the school. A Washington

15

newspaper had done a feature on him only a few weeks before.

Phoebe put her soda next to Janie and clambered over the bench. From across the table, Ted Mason gave her a smile and a casual wave. He was wearing an old polo shirt that had faded from dark blue to just the shade of his eyes. His curly brown hair was getting a little long. He'd been talking to Brenda Austin, who now smiled at Phoebe, too. In a striped jersey with hacked-off sleeves and tiny dangling gold earrings — three in her left ear — Brenda looked punk but casual. Despite the defiant attitude hinted at by her clothing, Brenda, the stepsister of Ted's longtime girl friend Chris, was a kind and sensitive, even serious, person.

"Hi, you guys," Phoebe said. "Where are Chris and Brad this afternoon? Off being presidential?" In the recent school elections, Chris had been voted student body president for next year, succeeding Brenda's boyfriend Brad Davidson, who was graduating in June.

"Chris is," Brenda replied. "She and Dick Westergard, the new vice-president, are planning how to computerize the student government budget."

"That's right, he's a biggie in the Computer Club, isn't he? Lots of luck to them; Brad used to complain all the time about the messed-up records he had to deal with."

As soon as the words were out of her mouth, Phoebe wished she could call them back. She was usually careful not to say anything around Brenda that might sound like she was flaunting her old relationship with Brad. They had gone together for over two years, before she fell in love with Griffin and broke up with him. Phoebe knew Brad was still a little resentful, but she had managed to overcome Brenda's wariness and was on good terms with her.

Brenda didn't seem to mind her reference to the old days. She said dryly, "He has bigger things on his mind now. The Princeton Alumni Club is having a party in Georgetown on Saturday, to give all the kids who are going there in the fall a chance to meet each other. At lunch today he showed me three neckties and asked me which one he should wear. As if I know anything about how Ivy Leaguers dress!" The others laughed.

"You should have let him borrow one of your funky T-shirts," Ted said. "Then he could have shown up in style."

"I would have," Brenda replied with a grin, "but he'd already made up his mind about everything but the tie. He doesn't want to be the only one there not wearing khakis, a blue blazer, and Weejuns, after all. First impressions make a big difference."

There was a note of irony, but no bitterness in Brenda's last comment. Brenda knew a lot about first impressions. When she first came to Rose Hill, after her mom married Chris's father, she gained a reputation for being wild and reckless that ended up bringing her a lot of grief. She was still living it down at school, but she got no hassles from her stepsister's crowd. They were her friends now, too.

"Which tie did he choose?" Woody asked. "The wide one with the pink flowers on it, or the one that says, KISS ME I'M IRISH?"

"Neither one. He went to Norton Farrier this afternoon to pick out a *new* tie and a shirt to match. Oh, and socks, too."

Woody whistled. "Norton Farrier! Will they let him in the door? I thought you had to be over fifty to buy things there."

There was laughter all around the table, and Phoebe turned to Peter Lacey. "Hey, Peter," she said, teasingly. "When are you going to find a new band to air on your show? You must be getting tired of playing nothing but Springsteen."

"Tired?" Peter was indignant. "Listen, when better records are made, the Boss'll make them! And I'll play them until you know *them* by heart, too."

"That's no promise, it's a threat," Woody said with a grin.

Peter ignored him. "Seriously, Pheeb," he continued, "give a listen to the show next Tuesday. I'm going to be interviewing the lead singer of a group I heard in Baltimore last week and playing their demos. What they do is mostly your basic three-chord rock, but wow! The singer sounds like Stevie Winwood when he was just starting out, and the drummer drives nearly as hard as Keith Moon."

"Really? I'll be sure to listen," Phoebe replied. She couldn't come up with a more intelligent remark. Peter had a way of assuming that everybody knew as much about the history of rock as he did. It was part of his total involvement with the subject. Griffin had been the same way about acting, tossing around names like Berghof and Grotowski and Adler as if she had the slightest idea what he was talking about.

That was part of being passionately interested in something, Phoebe knew. She wasn't involved in anything quite so seriously. She loved to sing, it was true, and she had just taken an important and scary step, starting voice lessons. But it wasn't her whole life. She didn't spend all her time practicing and learning new songs.

A feeling of loss flooded Phoebe's heart, but she pushed it away. There was no use regretting the trust she had placed in Griffin, in a relationship based on such a short acquaintance. How much time had they actually spent together? Did it add up to more than a day or two? She doubted it. But she had loved him, and he'd loved her. She knew that. He hadn't been acting. He couldn't help it if he put so much of himself into every role that he was bound to fall in love with his new leading lady.

Woody was watching Phoebe with concern, and she turned her face away. If she heard even one sympathetic word from him at this point, she was going to burst into tears.

"I wanted you to see this," Woody said cheerfully.

She glanced down. He was holding out a sheet of pink paper. She took it from him and saw at the

top, in big old-fashioned letters, the words CAST-
ING CALL. She read on. The Kennedy Players
were having auditions for their spring production,
an original drama written and directed by a student, Hugh Cromwell. Tryouts were the following
Tuesday at the playhouse. The last line of the
notice captured Phoebe's attention: FIND OUT IF
YOU HAVE WHAT IT TAKES TO BECOME A STAR!

Woody was looking at her with an expression
that was part amusement and part encouragement. "Hot off the presses," he said. "Since I'm
going to be stage manager, I'm supposed to pass
out these leaflets to promising actors and actresses. As far as I'm concerned, I just did."

"Me?" Phoebe asked. Woody nodded. She read
the flyer again. "It looks pretty tacky," she said
dubiously.

"The sophomore who designed it thought it was
eye-catching. Never mind the leaflet; what about
the audition? Like it says right there, this is your
chance!"

"I don't think I like acting," she said slowly.
"Or actors."

"Horsefeathers! You can't judge an ancient
and honorable profession by one person. *I'm* in
it, after all! Come on, Pheebarooni, give it a
shot. If you get a part, you'll have a fun way to
waste all your spare time for the next three or
four weeks, and if you don't get a part, you can
go home and waste your spare time writing a bril-
liant novel about how phony everyone in the
theater really is."

Phoebe could swear Woody could read her

mind. That was what true friendship was all about. He was offering her a chance to get her natural good spirits back in gear, but she wasn't sure that getting involved with theater herself might not just make her miss Griffin more. The last time she had been on a stage was to sing the sensational duet she and Griffin had performed for Woody's Kennedy Follies. She had fallen in love with him then and there, and what a folly *that* had turned out to be! Phoebe sat silently, lost in thought.

"Don't make up your mind too quickly," Woody joked. "The auditions aren't until next week."

"N–no," said Phoebe. "No, I won't."

Chapter
3

Cynthia murmured an apology as she brushed past a small group of people and hurried on down the hallway. She willed her feet to move faster, but much as she wanted to, she didn't break into a run. Her heart was pounding furiously, but on the surface she knew she appeared calm and cool, and together. She greeted some friends with a smile and a wave, and stopped for a moment to chat with a girl from her English class.

It usually took Cynthia all of the five minutes between periods to get from history to algebra. She estimated that this errand, and the detour it required, was going to add three minutes to her routine. No matter how she figured it, she was going to be late to class. Mr. McClure was bound to make one of his sarcastic remarks about tardiness, too. The later a student was, the more sarcastic the remark. It looked like she was going to set a new record this morning.

She knew this could have waited until lunch hour or even after school. A couple of hours one way or the other couldn't make the least bit of difference. But though her errand could wait, Cynthia couldn't. She had to get it over with. She'd spent the whole first period brooding about it, and hadn't heard a word of Mr. Sholeson's lecture on America in the Great Depression.

As she neared the cross-corridor, she slowed down to a saunter. Her breath was coming fast, but she did her best to give the impression of someone with all the time in the world and no particular place to go. As she turned right, she glanced around casually. She didn't see anyone she knew. The *Imagination* office, the third room on the left, was usually kept locked unless one of the staff members was inside working, but a wooden submission box hung on the outside of the door, always accessible to would-be contributors. Sharon O'Donnell, the editor in chief, wanted to make it as easy as possible for people to contribute to the magazine.

The pocket of emptiness in Cynthia's middle grew as she neared the door. She was mesmerized by the submission box, with its hinged lid and wide slot. She glanced around again, then reached into her notebook for the envelope.

For one awful moment she couldn't find it. Immediately she was sure that it had fallen out, either in class or in the halls as she rushed over here. Someone was sure to pick it up and open it. By lunchtime everybody in school would know about it! Then her fingers touched the envelope. Cynthia giggled at her own nervousness and fumbled the envelope into the slot. She turned away from the door with a heartfelt sigh of relief.

"Hi, Cynthia, how are you doing?"

Cynthia whirled, her heart thumping. Sasha Jenkins was standing there, smiling at her. With her long wavy hair, soft brown eyes, and Laura Ashley dress, she resembled a heroine on the cover of a romance novel.

Cynthia recalled her first impression of Sasha: She was much too pretty to be smart. It had taken only a few remarks by Sasha in class, however, to make Cynthia discover her mistake. And she realized, too, that she of all people should have known better. For as long as Cynthia could remember, people had been telling her she was cute. The soft, ruffled hair, her small face with its big eyes, freckled button nose, and dimpled cheeks, invited everyone to smile at her, pat her on the head — and then ignore her.

Cynthia didn't like being dismissed that way. She wanted to be taken seriously. By the time she reached high school, she had let people know that she was cute, yes, but there was a lot more to her than that. Some of her classmates thought she was a brain, but that was all right with Cynthia. When she spoke in class, people listened. And when her dimples *did* get the best of her, she couldn't help winning friends.

"Hi, Sasha," Cynthia said. Her voice squeaked anxiously. She wasn't positive that Sasha hadn't seen her put the envelope in the box. Better to give her an explanation just in case. "Um, I was just leaving a note for Bill."

"Oh? I thought you lived practically next door to him."

"That's right," Cynthia said quickly. "We were going to come to school together this morning, but I slept through my alarm. I had to rush like anything to keep from being late."

Sasha laughed. "I do that all the time! You handle it a lot better than I do, though. When I saw you in home room you looked totally cool and collected. What's your secret?"

Cynthia blushed. "S — secret?" she stammered. "Oh, I just — I guess I had a little more time than I thought I did." Pretty lame, Cynthia thought. I don't think I'm going to be much good at this cloak-and-dagger stuff.

Sasha was looking puzzled.

"Golly," Cynthia said abruptly, slapping the palm of her hand to her forehead. "There's the bell! McClure is going to massacre me! See you later!" She gave Sasha's arm a friendly squeeze and turned to escape.

"Let's have lunch together," Sasha called after Cynthia as she hurried away. "I've been meaning to tell you I liked what you had to say about *Catcher in the Rye* in class the other day. Maybe we can talk about Holden Caulfield!"

Cynthia waved an acknowledgment and started to run. Running in the halls was almost as grave an offense as being late to class, but not quite . . . not if the class was McClure's!

Her algebra teacher was in an especially good mood that morning. When Cynthia tried to creep into class unnoticed, he stopped lecturing just long enough to ask her whether the thing strapped to her left wrist was a particularly unattractive bracelet or a particularly inaccurate watch. Cynthia took her seat, opened her notebook, and tried to catch her breath.

Now that she had carried out her plan, she was starting to wonder if it was so smart. Sasha coming along at just that moment seemed to be fate's way of telling her that she was about to make a fool of herself. It probably wasn't too late to back out. If she rushed back to the *Imagination* office after class, the chances were that the envelope would still be in the box. She could take it out, tear it up, and no one — no one named Bill Magnuson — would be the wiser.

On the other hand, if she copped out now, she wouldn't be able to look at herself in the mirror when she brushed her teeth tonight. She had committed herself to a plan of action, and she was going to go through with it, and that was that!

The idea had come to her over the weekend. She had been riding her bike through the park, trying to concentrate on the wind in her face and the hiss of tires on the pavement rather than the feelings that were twirling like a tornado inside her. She wasn't sure how best to quiet the pangs of unrequited love. It sounded like a poetic condition, but somehow she didn't think that putting it all into rhymed couplets would make her feel any better. Writing poetry was usually the perfect outlet; this time, however, Cynthia thought a few fast sets of tennis — say fifty — might be more in order.

Cynthia had stopped pedaling, gliding to a stop near the old bandstand. Maybe she should give her art a chance to help her express and explore the confusion in her heart. There was no denying that hiding her feelings about Bill was putting a strain on her. She wasn't happy with the situation. A light and cheerful poem might be just the exercise she needed.

She'd begun to rough out a poem in her mind, and then imagined the new creation locked in her desk drawer with the rest of her poems. She had been pouring her thoughts and impressions and experiences into that drawer for years now. She expressed herself through her hidden poetry, sure, but the world at large didn't benefit from that expression.

On the other hand, the only person she could imagine showing her latest poem to was Bill! And she couldn't show it to him, for obvious reasons. The trap was so neat that it made her laugh.

"For every path into the forest, a path out of the forest." That saying was inscribed on a piece of parchment that hung in their front hall at home. Cynthia had always loved to trace the complex interwoven lines of the decorative borders and find the fantastic faces and animals concealed within them. Now it occurred to her that the

27

words themselves were more important than their appearances. Maybe she wasn't looking hard enough for her path.

She could send the poem of her hopeful, fearful love to Bill anonymously. As soon as she thought of this idea, Cynthia had rejected it with a laugh. It was too much like slipping an unsigned valentine card into somebody's desk. She wasn't in third grade! Besides, she knew Bill. If he got an unsigned poem in the mail, he'd get carried away playing detective, trying to figure out who had sent it rather than paying attention to what it said.

She had kicked the right pedal of her bike around into position and absently pushed off down the slope. Then she struck gold. If Bill got the poem as a submission to *Imagination*, it wouldn't occur to him that it was addressed to him personally. He always read the things that came in to the magazine carefully and responded to them as honestly as he could. She would be able to find out what he thought of both her writing and her situation, without having to make herself vulnerable.

By the time she had reached home, she'd composed a good part of the poem. By dinner time on Monday it was a polished piece. Cynthia used her dad's typewriter to make a clean copy of the poem and to draft the accompanying letter, which she planned to sign with an assumed name.

Deciding on a *nom de plume* had been practically the hardest part of forming her strategy, and she had to have a pen name or Bill wouldn't be able to write her in reply. She couldn't pick just any name, though. It *was* her poem, and she wanted the name of the poet to mean something personal to her.

She decided to use her own initials. She'd be bold enough to give Bill that much of a hint as to her identity. She started with "Charlotte" after Charlotte Brontë, and topped it with "Wodehouse," after the hilarious English novelist who wrote all the Jeeves books. As a final precaution, she looked in the phone book to make sure there wasn't *really* a Charlotte Wodehouse.

Cynthia had typed quickly, in amusement and anticipation. She'd give Bill something to think about!

> Bill Magnuson
> Poetry Editor
> Imagination
>
> ---
>
> Dear Bill Magnuson,
>
> I am sending you my poem "Shadow Dancer" to be considered for Imagination. I really want to hear what you think of it. If you leave your reply in the submission box, addressed to me, I'll be able to get it. Thanks for your time.
>
> Charlotte Wodehouse

Chapter 4

Cynthia put her change in her pocket, picked up her tray, and looked out into the crowded cafeteria. Peter Lacey's noontime rock show was already blasting from the speakers in the ceiling. The din of voices trying to make themselves heard over the music was almost deafening.

"Can I get by, please?" said someone from behind her. Cynthia apologized hastily and stepped away from the cashier's table. Usually she got to lunch in time to claim an empty table, where she would be joined by two or three friends she knew from her classes. Today, however, she was late. She couldn't keep herself from strolling past the *Imagination* office on her way to the cafeteria and peeking casually into the mailbox. Apparently Bill hadn't been by the office yet; her envelope was still in the box. She had to suppress an impulse to grab it. When a guy who was walking by glanced over at her, she smiled at him and jerked her hand back as if the mailbox had bitten her. She was sure she had the word "intrigue" written plainly across her face.

All the places at her usual lunch table were taken. Cynthia was wondering where to sit when she heard someone calling her. She looked around. From a table off to her left, Sasha was waving and pointing to the empty seat next to her. Cynthia started toward her, then hesitated. She liked Sasha and always enjoyed talking to her. They had had some stimulating conversations. But the table Sasha sat at was by custom reserved for the movers and shakers of the junior class. Cynthia didn't know them all that well and felt a little shy about joining them. But, what the heck. Cynthia smiled at Sasha and approached the table with a determined step.

She knew a couple of the boys, Woody Webster and Henry Braverman, from different classes; the others by sight only. One was Janie Barstow, the tall, slender girl who had been the star of the fashion show earlier in the year. She didn't seem at all stuck-up about it; if anything, she was on the shy and quiet side. Next to her sat Phoebe, the red-haired girl who'd helped emcee the fashion show, and Ted, the quarterback for the football team. He was certainly cute. Last was Brenda Austin, her nose buried in a big cup of soda.

"Hi, Cynthia," Sasha said, pushing an empty chair out from the table for her. "Do you know everybody?" Cynthia nodded, and received a variety of friendly greetings from the crowd. She didn't want them to break the flow of their lunch-time conversation out of deference to her, so she sat down quickly and turned to Brenda.

"You wrote that article for the newspaper last winter, didn't you?" Cynthia asked her. "The one about the halfway house in Washington?"

Brenda nodded warily. "Garfield House, that's right."

"I thought it was great. Everybody was talking about it for weeks."

Brenda relaxed visibly and smiled. "Really?"

"Sure. You made people feel as if they'd known the guy who runs it for years. He sounded terrific."

"He is." Brenda didn't bother to disguise the affection in her voice.

"I kept hoping to see more articles by you," Cynthia continued. "It was really one of the best things in the paper all year." She winked at Sasha. "Except for Sasha's articles, of course."

Everyone laughed. "I agree with you about Brenda's article," Sasha said. "After all, I'm the one who decided to print it. And I think she ought to write more, too. *The Red and the Gold* always needs good material."

"I will someday," Brenda mumbled, looking down at her plate, "when I have something else to write about that I think is really important."

Sasha laughed. "That's the difference between a writer and a journalist. I have to write about things whether I think they matter or not. Right now I'd rather be doing a piece on acid rain than an interview with the manager of a new chocolate shop at the mall. But the chocolate shop just opened, and it's a new advertiser, and that makes it news."

"How are the chocolates?" Henry asked.

"Devastating," Sasha replied, rolling her eyes. "And priced to match, of course."

"Better than granola?" Phoebe asked with a mischievous gleam in her eye. Cynthia knew that Sasha was something of a health-food nut.

"Better-tasting, sure, but not better for you." She paused to give her yogurt a stir and eat a spoonful, then turned to Cynthia. "Hey, before I forget, could I convince you to write an article on Salinger for the paper? Maybe something about why a thirty-year-old novel can still say something to kids our age. It would be just the right sort of thing for the Arts column I'm trying to get started. Cynthia has some very interesting things to say about Salinger," she explained to the others.

The sudden attention made Cynthia self-conscious. She said, "Yeah, maybe," directing the words into her macaroni and cheese. She knew that Sasha meant well, and part of her was soaking up the praise. But she wasn't confident enough about her ideas yet to commit them to print publicly.

When she looked up from her lunch, Cynthia was relieved to see that no one was watching her curiously or expectantly. Sasha's comment had offered her a chance to take the floor if she wanted it; the others at the table were ready to listen, but not to pry. They had moved on to new topics now, but were still including her. Cynthia had to admit to herself that it was fun to be accepted by the crowd. They weren't as intimidating as they appeared.

Sasha was talking to Janie about her boyfriend, Wes. "Four whole weeks somewhere in upstate New York, at a place called Fort Drum!" she said. "What burns me up is that he doesn't *have* to do it. He could just as easily hang around here and have fun."

"Then why doesn't he?" Janie asked.

Sasha made a face. "He says it's a chance to develop his leadership skills. I don't see why he needs to. I mean, he wants to be a Navy pilot. Pilots don't lead anyone, they just fly around in planes!"

Ted interrupted his conversation with Brenda to say, "If they're lucky! If they aren't — "

"Don't say it!" Sasha begged, real concern shadowing her pretty eyes. "Every time I look at a newspaper it seems like there's been another crash somewhere. And what Wes would really like to do is qualify for one of those stunt-flying teams. I feel sick every time I think of it."

"The Blue Angels?" Brenda said. "I saw them perform a couple of years ago, on the Fourth of July. It was really something. They were flying so close to each other it looked as if they could reach out and shake each other's hands!"

"I'd like it better if they just shook hands on the runway and then went out for coffee," Sasha replied. "It's not just the danger that bothers me, either. What those guys are really doing up there is practicing how to shoot each other down. If we

34

put half as much energy into trying to be friends with people in other countries as we put into getting ready to fight them, the world would be a lot better off."

There were a few nods, and a few skeptical looks, but no one volunteered to enter a political debate with Sasha. Woody began an imitation of a Blue Angel, making airplane noises and waving his arms menacingly, but glanced at Sasha and thought better of it. Instead he turned to Phoebe and embraced her, chair and all. He gave the pair of them a daring dip. Phoebe shrieked with laughter. "So how about it, Pheebarooni? Are we going to see you at the auditions this afternoon?"

"What auditions?" asked Brenda as Phoebe righted herself, pushing Woody aside playfully. "Are you going to try for a solo in chorus, Phoebe?"

"Not singing," Woody explained. "Drama. The theater. The temple of Thespis. The roar of the greasepaint, et cetera."

Phoebe pretended to smooth her ruffled feathers. "The Kennedy Players are having tryouts for their spring production this afternoon," she told Brenda.

"And Pheeb is going to be a star again," Woody added. "Right, kid? Come on, say yes! Tread the boards once more!"

Phoebe smiled reluctantly. "All right, I'll try out. But I don't know about this 'treading the boards' stuff. It sounds a little too much like 'walking the plank' for my tastes!"

The bell rang and the cafeteria sprang to life. Cynthia finished exchanging details with Sasha about the technical aspects of writing a piece for *The Red and the Gold*, and then joined the exodus toward the lunchroom doors.

On her way to the gym, she reflected on how much she had enjoyed lunch that afternoon. It had really taken her mind off the envelope in the *Imagination* mailbox, and she'd found Sasha and her friends good company.

The easy friendships the girls and guys shared reminded Cynthia of Bill and her, and for a brief moment she regretted the poem she'd written. But no, she thought to herself as she twirled the combination to her gym locker, she couldn't help wanting — wouldn't stop wanting — something even more special than a special friendship.

Chapter
5

Phoebe stopped just inside the entrance of the Little Theater. The former chapel was dark, but for the brightly, almost glaringly, lit stage. She narrowed her eyes against the light and saw a boy standing at center stage, looking back and forth between some invisible object in his outstretched right hand and a sheaf of stapled pages in his left.

"Can this be the book she meant?" he demanded fiercely. *"Can it?"* He paused, blinked, and looked around as if he expected someone to answer him. When no response came, he brought the script a little closer to his face and continued.

"Many have praised these words and pages," he said, sweeping his arm wide on *many* and pointing emphatically at the invisible book on *pages*, "but not *I*!" The pointing finger turned on him and stabbed him in the chest. "To me they smell nothing but foul *betrayal*!" He ended with a shout, his clenched fist pummeling the air.

A voice spoke from the darkness. "That's 'spell' nothing but betrayal, not 'smell.' Okay, thanks, um, Andy. The castings will be posted on the bulletin board on Thursday or Friday. Next?"

Phoebe peered into the auditorium. About halfway down, a table had been set across two rows of seats to create a desk at which three silhouetted figures sat. Five or six more people were scattered around the theater.

This was supposed to be a cure for her bad mood? What a joke! It was about as sad a scene as she could imagine. That poor kid Andy was going to spend the rest of the week berating himself for misreading one word, when in fact he was such a bad actor that he never had a hope. Phoebe was about to slip back out of the theater when one of the silhouettes at the makeshift desk rose and hurried up the aisle toward her. It was Woody.

"Hi," he whispered excitedly, "where have you been? I was starting to think that you were chickening out."

"I think I am," Phoebe whispered back. "I'll talk to you later."

As she turned to leave, he grabbed her sleeve. "Oh no you don't," he said in a normal voice. From behind him came a chorus of shushes. "Oh no you don't," he repeated in a whisper. "You promised! I told Hugh I'd talked you into trying out. Anyway, what'll it cost you to get up there and read a few lines?"

"About smelling betrayal?" she responded.

"Smelling *foul* betrayal," he corrected. "Actually, I like that better than the original, don't you? But never mind, you won't have to read those lines anyway. The speech Hugh's having the girls read is pretty good. Lots of scope to it. Do you know him?"

"Uh-uh."

He tugged at her arm. "Come on, I'll introduce you. He's dying to meet you. He's not just the director, you know; he wrote the play, too. He's very — well, come see for yourself."

Phoebe allowed Woody to tow her down the aisle. It was too late now to make waves. As they neared the row with the desk, Hugh called out, "That'll do for the reading, Will. Would you mind facing the right side of the stage? Now the other way? Okay, thank you. Check back at the end of the week." As a boy in a flannel shirt left the stage, he added in an undertone, "He has good presence. Too bad he can't speak above a whisper. I'll put him down for the crowd scene in Act II."

"Hugh?" Woody said.

Phoebe's eyes had adjusted to the gloom by now. As Hugh turned toward them, she was immediately intrigued by his striking looks. He had a firm jaw and a forbidding, unsmiling mouth. His deep-set eyes were shadowed by dark heavy brows, and above his high forehead a mane of thick dark hair crested wildly. He wasn't tall, but he was powerfully built, and he was very sharply dressed. He was certainly different from the average Kennedy senior.

"Hugh, this is Phoebe Hall."

"Of course it is," he said in a voice that hummed with power. "I'm glad you're here, Phoebe. I've wanted to meet you ever since I saw you in Woody's talent show last fall. You gave a first-class performance."

"Thank you," she said feebly.

"You think I'm flattering you," Hugh continued. "I hear it in your voice. You're wrong. I never flatter people. If we have a chance to work together, and I hope we do, you'll learn that for yourself. Are you here to read?"

"Well — "

"Good. Go backstage and take a few minutes to look over Helen's speech on page twenty-five. Karen," he said over his shoulder, "give Phoebe a script. I'll call you after the next person on the list."

Phoebe glanced around at the half-dozen others waiting to try out. She opened her mouth to say that she would rather wait her turn, but Woody grabbed the script from Karen and yanked Phoebe toward the aisle. Hugh was already watching the stage again as Karen called out, "Annie Burke? Onstage please, you're next."

"What did I tell you?" Woody whispered as he led Phoebe through the door to the dressing room area. "You've got one of the leads for sure!"

"I haven't even tried out yet," she protested.

"Pooh, that's just a formality. Hugh likes you and that's what counts. Unless you mess up royally, you're already cast. Here, here's your place." Woody flipped the script open to the proper page and took on a professional tone. "Read it over once for sense, again for stresses, and once more for places that might trip you up. Don't worry about the emotions. He'll set you up for it when you get out there."

Phoebe took the opened script and sat down on a pile of folded curtains. In the dim light, the blurry photocopied letters seemed to dance before her eyes. She put it down and pressed her fingertips against her eyelids. She wondered why she was doing this. It couldn't be just as a distraction.

Woody had helped talk her into it, of course. She wasn't exactly auditioning just to please him, but there was a little of that in it. A bigger reason was Griffin. Phoebe admitted to herself that she had something to prove, if only for her own satisfaction. Part of her still believed, deep down inside, that their successful performance at the Follies was entirely Griffin's doing. She had not had to act at all; she only needed to look at him and let all the love she felt appear on her face.

Of course he had been the stronger, the more accomplished partner. After all, he was a natural, a born actor. But if she could go onstage in this play, without him, and do a good job, it would show that what she had done with him had truly come from her.

She slid her fingertips from her eyelids to her temples and rubbed in little circles. It was only natural to be tense at an audition. Griffin had told her a real actor needs that tension to bring out his best. If he was right, she should be in good shape this afternoon; she had enough tension to start bottling it.

Phoebe tucked her hair behind her ears and pressed on her neck and shoulders with her fingers, tipping her head as far back as she could and moving her jaw from side to side. Finally she picked the script up from her lap and began to read Helen's part. After a few lines, Phoebe paused, furrowed her brow, and reread the passage. She *felt* what it meant, or thought she did, but she couldn't begin to make a direct translation of the haunting, evocative words. She read on and suddenly the meaning of the speech became clear.

Phoebe lowered the script and looked off into the distance. After a moment, she reached up and brushed a tear from her cheeks. At this point in the play, the character Helen was speaking of love and loss. The beauty and sadness of the scene caught in Phoebe's throat. This was so exactly what she was feeling! And Hugh Cromwell had written these words. He must be incredibly sensitive, as well as incredibly talented.

Phoebe had frozen in her chair. She couldn't possibly stand on a stage and say anything so intensely personal. These were words she might have spoken to Griffin. If she tried to utter them in front of strangers, their heat would weld her tongue to the roof of her mouth.

She couldn't do it, that was all. She would go back, hand Hugh the script, and tell him she had changed her mind. Too bad if he didn't like it.

She didn't owe him anything; she didn't even know him. He was certain to find someone else who was better for the part.

And Woody would be very disappointed; he might even be angry with her for letting him down after he had put himself on the line for her. Phoebe sighed.

Before she could come to a decision about auditioning, Phoebe was jolted from her reverie by Karen's voice calling her name. Phoebe gulped and stood up. It couldn't be her turn already!

"Phoebe? Oh, there you are! I guess you couldn't hear me through the curtain. You're on next." Karen peered at her curiously. "Are you okay? You look a little pale."

"No, I'm fine, it's just — "

"Good. Come on, Hugh is waiting." Karen said the name as if there were no other Hugh in the world.

Almost automatically, Phoebe followed Karen into the wings. The glare of the lights onstage brought her to a stop. She blinked, then glanced down at the script. The speech began, **HELEN:**. It was *Helen* who was speaking, not Phoebe. She could go out on the stage now and read this speech. She would not be reading it as herself. She would be pretending to be Helen, who had these experiences and feelings. If anything, the fact that she had similar feelings was a bit of luck. It meant that she would find it easier to convey what Helen was going through to the audience. She would be able to act more convincingly.

"Are you coming?" Karen prompted. "We've

43

got five or six more people to see after you."

Phoebe gripped the script tightly and took a deep breath. "Yes," she said. "Yes, I'm coming."

At center stage she stopped, faced the darkened auditorium, and waited.

"Now, Phoebe," Hugh called from the blackness, "you are a beautiful woman who is desired by many men, but the only one you love has just told you that he is in love with your bitterest rival. You feel betrayed, abandoned. In this speech you are trying to save some of your self-respect by telling him that he isn't responsible, that you have gotten yourself into the situation. Any questions?"

She shook her head. For a moment she stared down at her shoes, repeating to herself, I am Helen, not Phoebe. There is no Phoebe, only Helen. Then she began to read the lines. At first she was almost whispering, but as she went along, her voice grew stronger and more resonant. She tried to recall what her voice teacher had taught her about placement and breath control. By the end of the speech, she was still speaking in an intimate tone, but her words filled the theater.

After a brief silence, Hugh said, "Thank you."

The power drained out of her, leaving her feeling weak. She was turning to walk off when he added, "Would you mind turning to page eleven, Eve's speech near the top of the page? Eve is Helen's rival, and in this scene she is trying to win over Adam by pretending to push him away. He falls for it, but the audience has to know that she doesn't mean what she says."

Phoebe quickly scanned the lines, then read them out loud. She knew that it wasn't working, even before Hugh asked her to try the speech again. The sense of connection, of *being* the character, simply wasn't there. Phoebe walked offstage even before she heard the ritual "Thank you." She looked for Woody, and Hugh and Karen. She wanted to apologize to all of them for wasting so much of their time, and especially to Woody. She had let him down.

A hand reached out of the backstage gloom and grabbed her arm. "Hey, Pheeb," Woody exclaimed, "you were *fantastic*! You practically had us all reaching for our handkerchiefs! Listen, are you in a hurry to get somewhere? Can you hang around until we're done here? Hugh really wants to speak to you."

Numbly, Phoebe followed him out into the house. "All right, everybody, take five," Hugh called out. Woody motioned for Phoebe to take a seat in an aisle a few rows behind Hugh.

As Phoebe went to sit down, she found that the seat she had chosen was already occupied.

"Oh, excuse me," Phoebe said to the boy in the seat. It was too dark in the theater to see who it was. "I didn't realize there was someone sitting there."

"Don't worry about it, Phoebe," a familiar deep voice replied.

Phoebe took another look at the shadowed profile beside her. "Michael!" she exclaimed. Michael Rifkin was the son of Phoebe's music teacher, Miss Spinelli, and a new friend. Phoebe gave him a peck on the cheek. "What are you doing here?" she asked.

"Hugh asked me to write some incidental music for the play," Michael replied. "I knew you were a singer, but I didn't suspect you acted, too." Michael grinned broadly, and even in the darkness Phoebe could see his face light up with the smile. "Though I should have known. Anyone who can dance like you do should be a knockout on stage."

Phoebe smiled at his reminder of their one date. After her disastrous breakup with Griffin, Phoebe had decided to return her prom dress, since she and Griffin were supposed to have gone to the prom together. Michael had run into her when she was on her way to Saks. They hardly knew each other, but somehow by the end of their conversation she found herself agreeing to go to the prom with him. More than that, when the big night came she found herself having a good time.

At the end of the evening, though, the grief that had been hanging over Phoebe's head finally descended like an avalanche. Michael listened sympathetically to the whole story, then comforted her as best he could. Before she knew it, she was in his arms, kissing him with a passion that surprised them both. Her mind kept telling her that this instant attraction was all wrong, but it took all her will to pull away. When she told Michael that she wasn't ready to be involved with someone else, he had been disappointed, but still sympathetic and understanding. She appreciated his caring too much to feel awkward around him.

"It's good to see you, Michael." Phoebe was surprised at the warmth in her voice. "I'm glad you're here."

"Hey, what am I, chopped liver?" Woody's voice, from the seat next to her, caught Phoebe by surprise. "Michael, how are you doing?" Woody said, leaning over to shake Michael's hand.

"All right, everybody, quiet please," Hugh's voice rang out. "Let's get back to work."

"Phoebe, I've got to run," Michael said in a whisper as he got up to go. "You were great up there. That performance was as good as any you might see on Broadway." Phoebe flushed; she was sure this was a reference to Griffin. "I'll see you soon."

"Is Alice Lessing still here?" Hugh continued. "Alice, where are you?"

"Over here," a low, throaty voice answered.

"Are you ready? Will you give us Eve's speech in Act Three, please?"

Phoebe turned all her attention back to the stage.

Alice was a tall, slender girl with olive skin and long black hair pulled back in a ponytail. She was wearing a black leotard and a swirly blue peasant skirt. Phoebe remembered her now; they had been in Mr. Dodgson's math class together back in ninth grade.

As near as Phoebe could make out, Eve's

47

speech was about why men always have to be tricked into committing themselves to a woman. It was full of poetic images about goats on crags and antelopes bounding across the plain. What wildlife had to do with it, she couldn't have said, but it hardly mattered. The way Alice spoke the lines, Phoebe was ready to agree with anything she said. Her voice throbbed with conviction, and her face was filled with passionate intensity. When she reached the end, a couple of people started to clap.

"Thank you very much," Hugh said. He silenced the clappers with a glare, then looked back at the stage. "Can you wait a few more minutes, Alice? Karen, who's reading next?"

Three more students auditioned, but Phoebe was convinced that the two female leads had already been cast. She would play Helen, and Alice was going to be Eve. Alice was clearly a natural for the part. As for herself, she had no idea whether she'd read her lines well or not. Woody thought so, and he knew a lot about acting. But it was the way Hugh had spoken to her when she first came in that made her feel pretty sure she'd be chosen.

She had set out to prove that she could win recognition on her own, without Griffin's guidance and support. It looked as if she had just succeeded. Phoebe only wished she could feel happier about it.

In the heart of her satisfaction was a sore spot, like an aching tooth. She half-believed that in a crazy way, this role was a parting gift from

Griffin. The emotion she had put into reading the lines was a product of her experience with Griffin. She couldn't perform divorced from those feelings.

Phoebe was anxious, too, at the prospect of playing opposite Alice Lessing. She didn't consider herself a competitive person, but the dramatic circumstances would lend themselves to comparison. Everyone would be judging which of them was the better actress. It was built into the situation. Phoebe didn't have any overpowering drive to come out the winner, but she certainly didn't want to be the loser.

Chapter
6

Cynthia lay on her back in the grass, her head pillowed in her arms. The quad was quiet; she was alone with her thoughts. Her thoughts, however, were not as peaceful as her surroundings. She was still anxious about what Bill's response to her poem would be. It had been days and "Charlotte Wodehouse" still hadn't heard back from him. But Cynthia couldn't spend that much time feeling anxious. It was a lot more fun to fantasize about her first kiss with Bill. . . .

"Hello," a voice said.

Cynthia sat up quickly, grass and twigs scattering from her tousled hair. Brenda Austin was standing there giving her a tentative smile. "Oh, hi," Cynthia said warmly, brushing herself off and grinning.

Brenda let her leather shoulder bag slide off her arm to the ground, then sank gracefully to her knees next to Cynthia. "How've you been? I kept thinking I'd see you in the cafeteria again."

"It seemed too nice to stay indoors," Cynthia explained. "I've been bringing a sandwich from home and eating it out here in the quad."

She didn't add that she felt shy about sitting at Brenda's table again. It was easy the first time when she had been specifically invited by Sasha, who was one of the regulars. She didn't have the nerve to walk over there and sit down on her own.

Brenda leaned her head back, shook out her long dark hair, and closed her eyes. "Mmm," she said as the sun warmed her face, "I think you're right. It's *much* too nice to stay inside. I wish they'd cancel classes for the rest of the term and let us just sit around on the grass talking to each other. I bet we'd learn just as much . . . maybe more."

Cynthia smiled. "I was looking through some college catalogues the other day, and there must have been a hundred pictures of kids and professors in a circle on the grass. Do you suppose that's really what it's like?"

"Oh, sure, once or twice a year," Brenda said. She shifted her legs into a more comfortable position. "The rest of the time I bet it's just like here: sitting on a plastic chair in an ugly room, listening to the teacher go on and on, and trying to figure out if anything's important enough to write in your notebook."

"Or just trying to keep awake," Cynthia added with a laugh. "Sometimes the only way I can get through a class is by making up stories in my head. It can make any lecture easier to take."

"Oh, do you do that? I've always loved to make up stories, even when I was little. I wish I was a writer, so I could put some of them down."

Cynthia said in a puzzled tone, "But you are a writer."

"You mean that article about Garfield House?" Brenda shrugged. "I'll tell you a secret. I wrote that as a paper for one of my courses. My stepsister Chris gave it to Sasha without telling me. The first I knew about it was when I picked up *The Red and the Gold* and saw it there."

Cynthia gasped. "Really?" She would be horrified if someone took one of her poems and printed it without her permission. "Why did she do a thing like that?"

Brenda shrugged. "She thought she was doing me a favor. I was having a hard time fitting in around here, and she figured that seeing my name in the paper would give me a lift. For someone as intelligent as she is, Chris is pretty thick sometimes."

"You must have had a fit."

"Oh, I did. But it all worked out for the best in the end. There was this kid who had run away from home, a girl named Carla. She saw my article, just by accident, and went to Garfield House for help. She would have had a really rough time if she hadn't. I felt good about that; it kind of made up for the way I felt about Chris being so sure she knew what was best for me."

Cynthia nodded sympathetically. "I guess you

can never predict how you're going to affect somebody," she said. "I mean, you could just as easily not have heard about Carla. You could have changed her life without even knowing it, just by telling about something that was important to you. That's pretty exciting."

"I know." Brenda plucked a blade of grass and started to chew on it. "Maybe that's why I haven't written anything else. I'd be disappointed if I wrote something that didn't have any impact. And I'd be nervous, too, in case it *did* have an impact, but in the wrong way."

"But that's just it," Cynthia said with conviction. "We can't ever know all the consequences of what we do. And if we decide not to do something, that may have consequences, too. Who knows how many kids have been affected by *not* having the chance to read the articles you *didn't* write?"

Cynthia spoke the last lightly, but she believed in what she was saying. She was actually surprised at how strongly she felt about it. And it occurred to her that Brenda wasn't the only one who was holding something — maybe something special — back from the world. She thought of her own secret book of poetry.

Brenda had opened her mouth to reply, then glanced past Cynthia. A welcoming smile now lit up her face. Cynthia turned to look. Brad Davidson, the student body president, was walking across the quad in their direction. Cynthia had never spoken to him, but like everybody at Kennedy she knew who he was. He was tall and slim, with wide shoulders, brown hair, and friendly brown eyes, and as usual he was dressed as if he might unexpectedly find himself at a college interview. His maroon polo shirt fit him like a second skin, the crease in his tailored chinos was knife-sharp, and his cordovan loafers looked as if they had been polished that morning.

"Hi," Brenda called. "How you doing, stranger?"

"I couldn't find you in the cafeteria," he replied. "Then Ted told me he'd seen you out here."

"Uh-huh. It's too nice a day to stay indoors. You know Cynthia, don't you?"

Brad's political instincts took over. "Sure," he said warmly. "How are you, Cynthia?"

"Fine," she said with a smile. His tone was almost convincing enough to make her wonder if they were old friends and she'd just forgotten the fact.

"Sit down!" Brenda urged, looking up at Brad with mischievous eyes. "You can sit on my bag if you don't want to stain your pants."

"I would, but I've got to run. I really thought that once the election was over with, I could relax and let Chris deal with all this nonsense. No way; there's enough nonsense to keep Chris and me both busy. The latest crisis is about the Cardinal's Booster Fund. This yo-yo who's been acting as treasurer knows about as much about bookkeeping as your average chipmunk. Dick Westergard took the books home last night to try to make some sense out of them, and we're meeting now with Mr. Snyder to decide what to do about the whole business."

"I'll walk you over," Brenda said, scrambling to her feet. "There were a couple of things I wanted to talk to you about. See you later, Cynthia," she added. "I'll think about what we talked about."

Cynthia watched them as they walked across the quad. Halfway across, Brad reached over and took Brenda's hand. They were an unusual match, but somehow they fit together perfectly. Cynthia sighed. She and Bill had walked home from school together hundreds of times, but he had never held her hand or put an arm around her shoulders. She wondered if he ever would.

She glanced at her watch — just enough time to go by the *Imagination* office before her next class. She had been checking the mailbox for a reply to her poem three or four times a day since Tuesday, and she was beginning to wonder if she had been a fool to think that this was the way to get through to Bill.

After all, to Bill her poem was just another submission to the magazine. It could easily be a week or two before he got around to reading it. Even after he read it, he'd need some time to decide if he liked it and more time to write down his comments. With a sinking heart, Cynthia calculated that she might not get an answer before next *month*! And every trip she made to the mailbox increased the risk that he would catch her loitering there and figure out that she was Charlotte Wodehouse.

I'll indulge myself just once more, she thought as she got to her feet, and then I won't look again until Monday afternoon. And I'll do my best over the weekend not to bother Bill, so he'll have more time for reading.

As she neared the magazine office, her heart began to pound. That was another reason not to come looking so often. Cynthia was convinced that the repeated cycles of hope and disappointment weren't good for her health. She did her best to control herself, to feel calm and uninvolved. She pretended for a second that her friend Charlotte had asked her to check the submission box. Cynthia giggled.

Two kids approaching her from the other direction glanced at her, then looked again when they saw she was giggling to herself. She shrugged and smiled sheepishly. They walked on and the coast was clear. Her mouth was as dry as if she had just eaten a handful of saltines.

After a quick internal debate, Cynthia decided it was better to go directly to the box and open it in a businesslike manner rather than to flip the lid up casually as she walked past. If Bill saw her, either way would be just as revealing, and the average kid in the hall would take less notice if she looked like she had a right to do what she was doing.

Her hands were so damp that they slipped on the lid and it banged noisily back down with a clatter, but not before she had seen that there was something in the box. It could be anything, but it could also be . . . ! She wiped her palms on her jeans and opened the box again. Inside was a small white business envelope, not very thick. She gulped and turned it over to see, in Bill's familiar loopy handwriting, the name *Charlotte Wodehouse.*

For a long moment she stared down at it wide-eyed, then with a furtive gesture she stuck it into her book bag and hurried away feeling like a spy in an old movie. Now to find someplace where she could read it uninterrupted.

She looked again at her watch: barely five minutes until class! She was just passing the short hall leading to the front doors, and on an impulse she turned and left the building. She wouldn't go far, just to the flagpole out front. The broad granite base was usually crowded with kids before and after school, but this time of day it was mercifully empty. Cynthia sat down, took out the envelope, and swallowed several times. Then she pulled up the flap, took out the single sheet of white paper, and carefully unfolded it.

At the top of the page was typed a poem:

To a Shadow Dancer

You fear to show yourself in light
Or plainly tell of your delight
With one who doesn't know you care.
But why? How could he ever dare
To hurt someone for loving him?
To be loved unsought is not so grim!

Reach out to him and let him know
That he has set your heart aglow.
He may love someone else, it's true,
But still he'll warm to love from you.
If he can love you in return,
Your love need not in secret burn.

At the bottom, Bill had written, "I think *Shadow Dancer* is terrific! I want to print it in our next issue, right near the front where everyone will read it. I'll put 'by Charlotte Wodehouse' under it if I have to, but wouldn't you rather take the credit for such a wonderful poem? WHO ARE YOU? P.S. You can reply by way of the *Imagination* mailbox. A letter addressed to me and left here will be sure to reach me."

Cynthia laughed out loud. He liked it! He understood her poem. She felt a rush of affection for Bill, and then one of pride in her work. Bill liked her poem; what she had written was *good*. It looked like she was on her way to sharing her feelings with Bill.

She was certainly going to send him another poem. One or two lines were already drifting around in her mind. Lines that would make it very clear who it was that the shadow dancer loved.

Chapter
7

Phoebe was one of three or four aspiring actors standing in the lobby of the Little Theater after school on Thursday. When Woody walked in and saw her, he grinned and winked. Then he thumbtacked the scrawled cast list for Hugh Cromwell's play on the bulletin board and hurried away.

A glance at the list confirmed what Woody's face had told her: She had been given the part of Helen. Alice was cast as Eve, and the third lead, Adam, was going to be played by Art Blackstock. The name of the play, she learned from the page, was *Adam and Eve and Helen*. Not very original, but it gave an idea of what it was about, and the faint suggestion of fig leaves might help draw a bigger audience.

Just below the cast line was an announcement. A brief meeting of the entire cast would be held on Friday after school, to get acquainted and set up initial rehearsal schedules.

Phoebe was about to leave when she saw Alice hurrying toward her. "Is the list posted yet?" Alice called.

Phoebe nodded and smiled. "You're Eve," she said.

"Really?" Alice arrived at Phoebe's side and quickly scanned the list, as if she couldn't quite believe it. Her face glowed with pleasure. "Oh, thank goodness! I was so sure that I'd flubbed the audition!"

"Flubbed it? What are you talking about? You were terrific! Everybody thought so."

Alice laughed self-consciously. "It's nice of you to say so, but there were so many things. . . . But what about you, Phoebe? Will you be Helen? You ought to, if Hugh knows what he's doing."

It was Phoebe's turn to be self-conscious. "Yeah, I got the part," she said, lowering her eyes. "I hope I'll be all right. I've never done anything like this before, and I'd hate to make a mess out of it."

"Oh, you'll do fine! I saw you last fall in the Follies. I'm glad we're going to be working together. We'll have a lot of fun, I bet."

Privately Phoebe wasn't quite so sure. Something about Hugh told her that having fun wasn't part of his program for them. They'd find out soon enough. In the meantime, she was warmed by Alice's friendliness and encouragement. She couldn't help looking forward to getting started on the play.

"Say," she said to Alice, "are you in a hurry? Why don't we go over to the sub shop? Woody'll probably drop by when he's done here. Maybe we can talk him into giving us the scoop on our new director."

Alice nodded. "I'd like that," she said gravely. "It would be nice to get to know each other better, before we get too wrapped up in our roles."

At the sub shop, they found Ted and Peter chatting with another junior at the big table in the rear. Phoebe waved as she and Alice waited at the counter, but when their orders came, she led Alice to an unoccupied booth on the opposite side of the room. "I usually like hanging out with people," she explained, "but there's no way you can really talk to someone when there's a crowd around."

"This is just right," Alice said, sliding into the booth.

Phoebe took a bite of her sub. She remembered that Alice had an interest in art; that would be a good ice-breaking topic. "Do you still carry a sketchbook around all the time?" she asked before taking another bite.

Color flowed into Alice's olive cheeks. "I didn't think anybody noticed," she said.

"Oh, sure." Phoebe laughed. "I used to think it was really cool of you. Do you paint, too? I would love to have talent in that direction. I think I flunked fingerpainting in kindergarten, and it's been downhill ever since."

Alice smiled. "I try to paint," she admitted, "but I don't think I have a real feeling for it. Not like some of the kids I used to meet in art class, anyway. I guess I'm interested in too many things to be really deep down serious about any particular one. Sometimes I wonder if I'm missing out."

"Oh, so do I," Phoebe said. "I look around at the kids I know, and they all seem to have one involvement that just" — she searched for the right word — "*defines* them. I mean, look at Peter Lacey over there. You know him, don't you?"

"I know his voice," Alice said wryly. "Who doesn't?"

Phoebe laughed. "Well, he's a perfect example. The only things that matter to him are rock and radio, and he knows tons about both. He likes what he's doing, and he does it really well. Me, I just hack around."

"Oh, come on, what about music? You sing, don't you? You did a great number in the Follies with that gorgeous guy. Say, what ever happened to him? I haven't seen him around since then."

Phoebe winced. Alice had no idea that she was touching a sore spot. "Griffin Neill," she replied, making an effort to keep her voice level. "He dropped out of school to become an actor. He's playing one of the leads in a new production of *West Side Story* at the regional theater."

"He is? I'm impressed. But I didn't think he was any more talented than you. If *you* wanted to sing professionally, I bet you could do it."

Phoebe toyed with her sandwich and didn't say anything. Becoming a professional singer was a half-formed ambition that she was not yet ready to confess to anyone.

"And just think how lucky you are to have had that experience on stage," Alice continued. "I'm terrified that I'm going to do something dumb up there, like wander out before I'm supposed to, or trip and fall into the audience."

"Or walk out and suddenly realize that you don't know any of your lines," Phoebe said with a groan. "I know I'm going to have nightmares about that from now until the play is done with. Then there's the one where I open my mouth to sing and nothing comes out. Don't worry, Alice. You'll be great. Everybody has fears like that. The important thing is not to let them get to you."

"I know," Alice sighed. "I know. It'll be a lot easier, knowing there's someone in the cast who knows what I'm going through. Isn't it amazing what just a little sympathy and support can mean? Sometimes it makes all the difference."

Phoebe nodded. "Sympathy and support" pretty much defined Woody since her breakup with Griffin. She did know how important it was to have an understanding friend.

"I really envy kids who have sympathetic parents," Alice continued. "It must make everything so much easier. They don't have to spend all their time either trying to justify what they're doing or trying to hide it."

Phoebe nodded in agreement. She recalled the long conversations she'd had with her parents before they agreed to pay for voice lessons with Miss Spinelli. She had to persuade them that she was really serious about studying voice. And it hadn't been easy to do, especially since she wasn't completely convinced herself. But in the end they had agreed to let her give it a shot.

She told Alice about this. Alice made a face. "That isn't the way my parents would have acted, I can tell you. When I told them last week that I was trying out for a play at school, they spent most of dinner talking about how most actors end up driving taxis or waiting tables for a living. As if I was going to run off to Broadway over one audition."

Phoebe giggled. "I got something like that, too," she admitted. "My mom suggested that if I go through law school and get a job, I can always sing with a community chorus or something, and then I won't have to worry about whether soloists are paid enough to buy groceries."

"Is your mom a lawyer?"

"No, my dad is. What do your parents do?"

"My dad works for a company that makes paper plates and stuff, and my mom has a little gift shop at Mill Creek Mall."

"Really? Maybe I've been there — what's it called?"

Alice smiled sheepishly. "It's called Lessing Gifts," she said. "That's my last name, Lessing.

"I don't think I've noticed it," Phoebe said.

"Most people don't. It's on the second level, between Milovan's and the waterfall. Porcelain birds are her biggest seller. Would you believe that some people collect hundreds of them? Those and little statuettes of kids in peasant costumes."

"My aunt collects them," Phoebe replied. I know what you mean. They are a little bit much."

The two girls ate in silence for a few minutes. Then Alice asked, "Have you read Hugh's play yet?"

"No," Phoebe said. "Only the bit he had me read at the audition. Why, have you?"

"Oh, no. I just thought that since you're such a good friend of Woody's, he might have lent you a copy of the script."

"No, I don't know anything more about it than you do," Phoebe said with a shrug. "I guess we'll get copies at tomorrow's meeting."

"Tomorrow? When tomorrow?"

"Right after school. Didn't you see the announcement? It was at the bottom of the page with the cast list."

"I didn't look," Alice confessed. "The only thing I saw was my name at the top. What am I going to do?"

"What's the problem?" Phoebe was concerned by Alice's distress.

"I told Mom I'd help at the store tomorrow afternoon while she's talking with sales reps. I don't know how I'm going to get out of it. Wouldn't it be awful to miss the very first meeting?"

"You'll just have to tell your mother that the demands of art come first," Phoebe said with a straight face.

Alice looked at her as if she thought Phoebe might be serious, then cracked up. "She'd love that." Alice rolled her eyes. "She'd have a stroke.

No, I'll tell her I've got a date at the soda fountain with the captain of the football team. That should be all-American enough for her."

Phoebe laughed. "Modern-day parents. They just don't always understand that life these days isn't like an episode from *The Brady Bunch*!"

"Or *Happy Days*."

"Or *The Partridge Family*."

The two girls giggled.

"Actresses!" Phoebe threw her hand to her forehead dramatically. "We have it rough."

Chapter
8

Cynthia woke early on Saturday morning firmly convinced that all was right with the world. Golden sunlight streamed through the window and pooled on the floor. A flower-scented breeze stirred the curtains. In the front yard, birds carried on a lively conversation from the branches of the old lightning-scarred oak. From downstairs came the aroma of her dad's weekend special, blueberry pancakes and bacon. That was one breakfast she never slept through. She stretched and sighed happily.

After a three-minute shower, she pulled on a pair of khaki shorts and a pale yellow boat-neck T-shirt and ran down the stairs. Her mother was at the breakfast table, sipping a cup of coffee and browsing through a medical journal. She looked up and smiled. Cynthia poured herself a glass of orange juice and sat down across from her.

From near the stove, her father said, "Hi, honey. Are you ready for a short stack? I flipped these just for you."

"Sounds fantastic, Dad." Cynthia took the plate of pancakes and began to apply butter and syrup. There was a real art to it. Some people might be satisfied to put a pat of butter in the middle of the pancake and let it melt however it liked, but not Cynthia. She carefully spread butter across the whole surface of each pancake, then poured the syrup in a spiral, beginning at the middle. Perfect. She put the first heavenly bite in her mouth.

"How was your week?" her mom said, putting aside her magazine. Saturday mornings Cynthia and her parents got caught up on each other's news.

"Okay." She was about to add that a poem of hers had been accepted by the school literary magazine, but she stopped herself in time. She'd have to give them some explanation about the pen name and then it would be just too easy for one of them to let the cat out of the bag next time they talked to Mr. or Mrs. Magnuson. No, they'd be proud of her, sure, and she'd love to share her success with them, but it was just too risky. Cynthia devoted herself to her pancakes, using that as an excuse not to elaborate on the latest school gossip.

"I dropped by the Albatross Bookshop the other day, looking for the new Philip Roth, and had a chat with a friend of yours," her mother continued.

"Oh, Sasha? She was one of your patients, wasn't she? That's her parents' store."

"I know. Well, they've got a sweet, bright daughter. I really enjoyed talking to her. By the way, she had some very complimentary things to say about you. She told me that she's been trying to get you to work on the school paper."

"Oh well," Cynthia said modestly, "she's just saying that. I'm not the reporter type."

"Maybe not, but I gathered she wanted you more as a columnist. It might be a lot of fun."

"Here we are," Mr. Walker announced, "a stack for me, a stack for Mom, and a little bonus for our Cindy!" He put the plates down and began to fix himself a cup of coffee. "What's all this I hear?" he added. "Are you going after a Pulitzer Prize now, lambkins?"

"Dad, really — lambkins! I'm not five years old anymore."

"I know," he agreed, "but from the perspective of my advanced years, it doesn't seem all that long ago that you *were* five. If it'll ease your mind, I solemnly pledge not to call you lambkins in mixed company. I also promise not to show prospective suitors your baby pictures."

"Gee, thanks, Dad. You're too kind." Cynthia knew her dad wasn't trying to make fun of her by talking about suitors when she'd never even had a boyfriend — it was just a dad-type of thing to say. She decided not to hold his eagerness to consider her belle of the ball against him.

"Robert," Mrs. Walker said in a no-nonsense

voice, "don't tease. Your hotcakes are getting cold."

"So they are," he replied, and forked a bite. "Mmm. Nothing like coldcakes and bacon for breakfast, followed by a nice cup of lukewarm coffee."

Cynthia took his coffee cup and put it in the microwave to warm up. "Good daughter," Mr. Walker said. From the table, her mother asked, "Has Sasha mentioned the picnic to you yet?"

"No. What picnic?"

"She told me that she's trying to organize a picnic in a couple of weeks, down by the old canal. The Park Service has put in several new picnic areas along the towpath, you know."

"Oh. No, she didn't say anything. But then I haven't seen much of her these past couple days."

"Well, she made it very clear that she likes you and would like to be even better friends with you. If she hadn't asked you about the picnic yet, there's probably a good reason. She said she was looking forward to seeing you there. I already volunteered to make a fruit salad for you to take along."

Cynthia leaned her elbow on the table and rested her chin on her hands. A glow of excitement stole into her eyes. "It sounds like a great time, Mom, and your fruit salad is sure to make me the most popular person there. I really do like Sasha, and I'm finding out that her friends are a really fun group." Cynthia started calculating in her mind who would be at the picnic, and she suddenly wondered if it was going to be the kind of thing where you had to have a date. She contemplated the subject while she rinsed her plate and glass at the sink. "I'm going out for a ride," she called back to her parents as she left the kitchen. "Be back in an hour or so."

Cynthia wheeled her red and gold ten-speed out of the garage and hopped on. The bike was an old friend — she'd taken good care of it since she got it five years ago, and with any luck it should last another twenty. She patted the handlebars fondly as she rolled down the driveway.

On an impulse she turned left from her house and rode toward Park Heights. This exclusive part of town had more hills to contend with, but the streets were shadier and quieter, and there was the little-used Rosemont Park for a destination.

She loved the view of the Potomac valley from the highest hill of the park, a former estate. Cynthia sat on a rustic bench that circled the trunk of a huge maple and leaned back to catch her breath after the stiff climb. The bark felt rough through her thin shirt. The energizing bike ride had cleared her mind; now the thoughts came tumbling back in.

Her new poem was sitting in her desk drawer, waiting to be typed. It was the partner to the first poem and she'd called it *Dance Into the Sun*. In it, the shadow dancer mused about what would happen if she came out of hiding, unsure as to whether the contact with the one she loved would scorch her like the burning sun or bring her new life.

Cynthia thought it was a good, honest poem; she was almost certain Bill would like it as much as Charlotte Wodehouse's first. She was reminded suddenly of the conversation she'd just had with her parents at breakfast, and the possibility of Bill discovering the mystery poet's identity. She was positive he didn't know that it was her. If he knew, he could never hide the fact from her. She would read it in his face, that is if he didn't come right out and demand to know what she was up to. "Who's the lucky, guy, Cyn?" And that was assuming that he couldn't tell, just by looking at her, that she was helplessly in love with *him*.

Cynthia tried to recall the last expression she'd seen on Bill's face, since he read the poem. She was well aware that she hadn't even seen him since the day she surreptitiously dropped that first poem in the submission box. Each day she had walked home directly instead of hanging around waiting or looking for him. Lunches she had spent on the quad. She hadn't dropped by his house in late afternoon either, as was her longstanding custom. He must be starting to think she was avoiding him for some reason.

Cynthia suddenly sat up very straight. The blade of grass she had been chewing on fell out of her mouth unnoticed, adhering to her chin. She *was* avoiding him! She was in love with Bill, and she was avoiding him. That makes a lot of sense, kiddo, she thought wryly. Absence makes the heart grow fonder — ha.

But avoiding Bill did make sense, she realized, if she thought that he could read her face, just as she was sure that she could read his. It wasn't so farfetched a possibility; they had known each other a long time. If nothing else, he would certainly notice that she was more restrained than usual. From there it was a short step to wondering if she was keeping something secret from him. And from there it was no distance at all to suspecting that her secret and his mystery were related.

Still, it wasn't very nice of her to stay away like this. She brushed the piece of grass from her chin. He might think she was mad at him or something. Besides, she missed him. She wanted to be with him. Among other things, she was curious to find out if he was invited to Sasha's picnic. Maybe he'd suggest they go together. Maybe *she'd* suggest it. It was a scary but wonderful thought.

Cynthia coasted back down the path to the park entrance, relishing the wind against her face. She decided to swing by Bill's house right now. It was still a little before ten, but Bill was an early riser. He had probably been up for hours. He might already have tried to call her and she was out on a bike ride! They had been talking for weeks about canoeing on the C & O Canal. Of course, he had looked out the window this morning and decided it was the perfect day for it. He was probably on the phone at that very moment, trying to find someone to take her place.

She was still coasting downhill on a gently winding, smoothly paved path. She changed to a higher gear and began to pedal. Her tires screeched on the asphalt and the wind forced tears from the corners of her eyes. Riding like this she could be home in five minutes. If Bill had left a message with her parents, she might be in time to call him back and catch him before he went.

Suddenly she recalled the short flight of steps at the foot of the path, just before it joined the gravel drive. She couldn't jump them at this speed. Even if she somehow managed to, she couldn't land on gravel and hope to stay in control.

She grabbed for the brake levers and squeezed them, rear brake first. The bike slowed slightly, but seemed determined to continue its downhill plunge. Cynthia squeezed harder, trying not to look at the concrete steps that were coming up so fast. She was not going to stop in time.

Cynthia turned the handlebars, swerving around the steps onto the grassy slope beside them. She felt the tires start to slide, then regain their hold. An instant later, the ground dropped away. She clutched the handlebar grips tighter, fighting to keep the front wheel pointed straight. The impact knocked the breath from her, but she was on the gravel now and still upright. Tempting fate, she threw the bike into a sideways skid and stopped in a cloud of dust.

Now that she was safe, Cynthia was terrified. Her knees had dissolved and she was gasping for breath, her heart thundering. She looked back. The hill she had just careened down looked about as steep and as high as the Eiffel Tower. She chided herself for riding so recklessly, and all because Bill might be trying to call her. She was definitely crazy. First she spent the whole week avoiding the guy, then she nearly broke her neck trying to get to him.

Cynthia stood with a foot on the ground on either side of the bike, leaning on the handlebars with her head on her arms. She breathed deeply. Why don't I just give up, she thought. What good am I doing myself by hoping that my silly poetry will make him love me? He doesn't even know who "me" is. He thinks I'm Charlotte Wodehouse. And he thinks Charlotte Wodehouse is . . . oh, I don't know!

Cynthia stood up and hitched herself onto the bicycle with a sigh. I know why I won't give up, she said to herself. If I do, I'll never know if Bill really might like me. And he won't know that I'm ready to like him back, as much as he'll let me. There's nothing for it but *Dance Into the Sun*. It's all up to you, little poem number two!

Cynthia felt calm enough now to resume her ride home, at a safer pace needless to say. Turning onto her block, she saw Bill in his front yard wearing cut-off jeans and sneakers, playing with his puppy Rags. Nice legs, she first thought. So much for canoeing on the canal, she thought second.

Bill saw her and waved. She swung into his driveway, parked the bike, and walked over to him.

"Hi," he called, "where have you been all my life?"

75

"I rode up to Rosemont Park. I love the view from the top."

"Uh-huh. I have spent the morning trying to teach this sad excuse for a dog to do a couple of tricks. Want to see the results?"

He had a stick in his hand, and now he held it out horizontally, about six inches off the ground, and said, "Okay, Rags, jump!"

The puppy looked at him, looked at the stick, and wagged his tail. Then with a miniature growl he lunged forward and grabbed the stick in his teeth, trying to back away with it. When Bill resisted, he growled louder and dug his front paws into the turf, jerking his head, and the stick, from side to side.

"See what I mean? Isn't that great?" Bill released his hold. Rags, surprised by his easy victory, tumbled backward, then bounced up and offered the stick to Bill. He took it and said, "That's not all. Watch this. Okay, Rags, *fetch!*"

The stick went end over end through the air and Rags tore out after it. The puppy overshot, but quickly whirled around, picked up the stick, and trotted triumphantly toward them. Cynthia was about to clap when Rags stopped four or five feet away, wagged his tail, and looked at Bill challengingly.

Bill put out his hand for the stick. The puppy backed away. Bill took a step toward him. The puppy turned, ran a few steps, then looked back to see if Bill was following him. When Bill pretended to walk away, the puppy tagged behind him but watched alertly for any attempt to grab the stick.

"This is hot stuff, huh?" Bill snorted. "I'm thinking of letting Ringling Brothers, Barnum and Bailey in on the act."

Rags, noticing that he had lost his master's attention, came over and dropped the stick in favor of chewing on Bill's shoelaces.

"Ha!" Bill exclaimed, and grabbed the stick. "Fooled you, you miserable beast!"

Cynthia knelt down and fondled the puppy's ears. "Don't listen to him," she whispered to the puppy, giggling as Rags licked her face. "He's really not so bad, as long as you do things his way."

"Are you trying to poison my dog's mind against me?"

"Oh no," she said demurely. "I'm just trying to help him understand you."

"Same thing." Bill laughed and squatted down to scratch the dog's tummy. "Anyway, he's the one that needs understanding, not me."

"*I* understand him. It's a simple vocabulary problem. He thinks 'jump' means tug-of-war and 'fetch' means catch me. You're speaking the wrong language, pal!"

"Great! I spend the week reading stories and poems by kids who don't have a grasp of simple English, and on weekends I get to play with a dog that has the same problem!"

Cynthia had heard this kind of comment from Bill many times before, but now the Charlotte

Wodehouse in her was taking it personally. She felt herself puffing up with indignation. "You must get a few good things now and then, don't you?"

"Oh sure," he admitted. "As a matter of fact, I made a real discovery this week. Someone named Charlotte Wodehouse turned in a poem that is just fantastic. I was so blown away by it that I've been carrying it around in my notebook. Sometime I'll have to show it to you."

Cynthia studied his face, she hoped casually. He didn't seem to be playing a game with her. "Charlotte Wodehouse?" she said. "I don't know her."

"I'd be surprised if you did. There's nobody by that name in the student handbook, and it's obviously a pen name. I wish I could find out who she is. There was something about her poem that fascinated me. This may sound corny, but I feel like I have a kind of bond with her."

Cynthia felt as if a hippopotamus had just sat on her stomach. She thought her heart would burst. He was beginning to be aware of the special feeling between them, too! Of course he didn't know that she was Charlotte Wodehouse, but her poem had touched him just the way — no, far more than — she had hoped it would.

Cynthia was wondering how to tell him the truth, already feeling his arms around her, when he continued. "Part of it's the mystery, of course. It's like getting a crush on someone you only know from seeing her in class. You know you like her looks, and you can imagine that her personality is pretty much any way you like."

"Until you meet her," Cynthia pointed out.

"Right. She might turn out to be a total witch."

"Then maybe you shouldn't try to meet your mystery poet."

He shook his head. "No, someone who has that kind of beauty in her has to be special. You know, Cyn, I'm really lucky to have you as a friend. Who else could I talk about such crazy stuff with? Falling in love with someone after reading a poem she wrote. Most people would think I'd gone right off into the twilight zone! But you understand, and you don't think I'm a flake because of it. That's very important to me."

"Bill — " she began, then closed her mouth. How could she confess to him now? He would be sure that she had deliberately tricked him into talking like this, and he would hate her for it.

He misunderstood her silence. Clapping her on the shoulder, he said, "I didn't mean to embarrass you with all the mushy stuff. Friends forever, right, kiddo?"

"Right," she said with a sinking heart.

Chapter
9

"What does he want with us?" Alice asked.

"I don't know," Phoebe grumbled, "but I hope it's important. My dad and I had a date to play tennis this afternoon. He was really disappointed when I cancelled on him."

"Huh!" Alice replied. "You should have heard what my mom had to say. I usually help out in the shop on Saturdays. That's the busiest day at the mall."

They were sitting on the steps of the Little Theater waiting for Hugh. After the meeting on Friday he had taken them aside and told them that as the leads they would be carrying most of the weight of the production. He wanted them to have special preparation and was planning to devote extra time to working with them. He concluded by ordering them to be at the theater the next day at two. Alice had started to object, but something in Hugh's look made her swallow her protest.

A beat-up orange Volkswagen convertible with its top down bounced into the parking lot and screeched to a halt. Hugh vaulted out without opening the door and hurried up the walk toward them.

As he drew closer, Phoebe was struck once again by the intensity of Hugh's face. He was handsome, but not in a way that invited familiarity. He was too completely in control. Now his eyes gleamed with a barely tamed energy. There was danger in them, she knew, but it was like the danger of a roller coaster, attractive *because* it was dangerous.

He stretched out a hand to each of them and said, "I'm glad you both could come." Phoebe forgot the words she had been rehearsing on the subject of his tardiness and let herself soak up the warmth of his gladness. "We have so much to do, so much to learn," he continued, "and always so little time."

As he unlocked the door to the Little Theater, he added, "In Europe there are special schools for those who intend to enter the theater. All their studies are directed toward their profession. Stagecraft, diction, body alignment, fencing . . . the well-prepared actor needs all of those and much, much more."

Alice and Phoebe waited just inside the door. Hugh kept talking as he vanished into the darkness, heading in the direction of the stage. His voice surged and faded like a too-distant radio station. ". . . few weeks, but with dedication and hard work we can. . . . that moves and lives. Just a second, here we are — " Like the climax of a magic show, the stage suddenly blossomed into light. Hugh stepped out from the wings, made a wide gesture of invitation with his arms, and said, "Are you ready to work?"

Phoebe and Alice climbed the rickety set of temporary stairs that stood at one side of the apron. They joined Hugh on stage and took two of the rusty folding chairs he had set out. He picked out the third, turned it around and straddled it, leaning his arms on the back. "I've read a lot of authorities on the proper preparation for an actor," he said, motioning to a stack of books on the floor next to his chair. "All of them agree that it takes years. We don't have years, though, or even months."

"Three weeks," Phoebe agreed.

He ignored her remark. "What I'm going to try with you two is to work intensively on the most crucial aspects of your training and rely on your natural talents to carry the rest. And make no mistake about it: Both of you are *very* talented. I wouldn't have picked you otherwise."

Phoebe reacted strongly to this unsolicited testimonial. She often doubted her own abilities. When people had complimented her on her performance in the Follies, she had told them that she owed it all to Griffin, and what's more, she had meant it. Now, to hear an expert like Hugh say that she was not just talented, but *very* talented, made her want to stretch and purr like a stroked cat.

At the same time, however, she sensed the faint, distant stirrings of resentment. Hugh's words almost suggested that *he* was somehow responsible for their talent. He might have a lot to teach them — she certainly hoped so — but she and Alice and the others were still the ones who had to go out on stage in front of an audience and play their roles. She was no glory hound, but she believed in credit placed where it belonged.

Woody had once made a joke about a teacher they both disliked: "If we flunk Mr. Skenk's course, it proves we're lazy and stupid, but if we do well it proves he's a fantastic teacher." She hoped that wasn't going to be Hugh's attitude. But maybe she was being unfair to him. Better to withhold judgment until she knew him better.

"We'll begin with a very simple exercise," Hugh was saying. "Here, take these." He handed them each a book. Phoebe glanced at the title of hers: It was called *Six Steps to Acting*. Alice was holding a book with a similar title. Phoebe was beginning to thumb through her book when Hugh continued. "Lie down on your back with the book under your head and neck."

Phoebe looked dubiously at the dusty stage but she did as she was told.

"Now slide your feet toward your body until your knees are about half-bent. Let your arms rest on the floor. That's right, good. Close your eyes and breathe slowly, in . . . and out. Feel the breath spreading into your chest, and your back, expanding your ribs. Now find your center and feel the energy flowing outward. It's flowing through your shoulders and arms, and out your fingertips. Feel the energy spreading down through your legs and feet, and out through the the tips of your toes."

To her astonishment, Phoebe did feel a kind of warmth spreading outward from just below her rib cage. Her breathing became deeper and slower. The beating of her heart sounded loud in her ears.

Hugh was almost whispering now. "Let yourself sink into the floor. All the weight is falling away from you and you are floating in an empty space. Now send your awareness throughout your body. Look for the little knots of tension and tell them to go away. Relax your toes . . . your feet . . . your calves. . . ."

As he worked his way up the body, Phoebe found it harder and harder to concentrate on his words. She wouldn't even try. She'd just relax, just as he had said, and let the drowsy warmth float her away.

"All right," Hugh suddenly said in a normal tone of voice.

Phoebe's eyes flew open. Had she fallen asleep? For how long? It might have been a minute or an hour; she had no idea at all. She only knew that she felt wonderfully rested and clearheaded.

"Before you sit up, take some mental notes. How did it feel to have all the parts of your body in their proper relationship with each other? You can recapture that feeling whenever you need to. If you feel yourself bunching up from stress or nervousness, just grab a book, lie down on the floor, and put yourself back into alignment. At the theater where I apprenticed, the whole company did this before every performance."

Phoebe wondered where Hugh had apprenticed. Griffin could probably tell her — Then she remembered that she wasn't going to be seeing Griffin or talking to him, ever.

Phoebe shut her eyes in misery. It was no use. She would never really be properly "aligned" again. Her shoulders were tensing, hunching inward and upward toward her ears. In about three minutes she was due for a killer headache, and she knew there wasn't any aspirin in her bag.

Suddenly Hugh leaned over her, placed his hands under the back of her head, and gently pulled. Surprised, Phoebe resisted; then she allowed her neck muscles to relax. Magically the tension drained away from her shoulders.

Her neck tingled where Hugh's fingers touched her. Phoebe felt a strange thrill to think that he might massage her shoulders next. She wasn't entirely sure that she should let him, but she reasoned that this was part of her training. And he was making her feel better — she had no cause to object.

She didn't have a chance to. Hugh put a tiny bit more pressure on her neck muscles, then carefully replaced her head on the book and took his hands away. She missed them at once. When she heard his footsteps move away, then stop, she opened her eyes and looked around. He was kneeling next to Alice now, cradling her head in his palms and talking to her in a low murmur.

A sudden spurt of anger ran through Phoebe. It shocked her. She and Alice were becoming friends, and she hardly knew Hugh at all. It was ridiculous to be jealous of Hugh's attention to Alice. Before Phoebe could begin to analyze her aggressive, uncharacteristic reaction, Hugh stood up and said, "That exercise was to help you become more aware of yourselves. The next one is aimed at helping you become more aware of one another."

He stretched out a hand to each girl, and tugged them to their feet, then placed them facing each other at a distance of about a foot.

"For now," he continued, "all I want you to do is look into each other's eyes. Let your awareness grow and flow into the other person. Don't force it or try to guide it. There is nothing to figure out, no problem to solve, just the two of you entirely in the present. . . ."

Alice's face seemed blank at first, but then Phoebe began to see it as serious, even searching. She found it oddly difficult to keep looking at her. She had to fight the impulse to look away, to blink, to yawn, even to giggle. What gave her the strength to go on was the thought of how hurt Alice might be if she did any of those things. And she very much didn't want to disappoint Hugh.

His voice broke into her concentration. "Now listen carefully: I want you to mirror on your face the feelings that you sense in the other person's eyes. You are no longer separate people, you are linked in a circle of shared understanding. Bring that understanding to the surface. Let it reach out to those of us who are not part of your circle."

Phoebe sharpened her gaze, as if she could literally bore through the other girl's eyes into her mind. There was a happy gleam there, a joy at being here in this empty theater, stretching herself in ways that her ordinary life never stretched her. What a change it was from the frozen life of the statuettes in her mother's store, what a happy change from her lonely sketching expeditions. Phoebe's lips softened into a smile that spoke of both expectation and fulfillment.

At that moment, to her dismay, she saw Alice's eyes fill with tears and her face draw into a perfect mask of tragedy. Phoebe reached out to touch her shoulder, and suddenly the other girl was sobbing in her arms. Phoebe held her and comforted her just as she would have comforted her little brother Shawn.

"I'm sorry," Alice said, stepping back and brushing the wetness from her cheeks. "It's very silly of me, but when I looked in your eyes I saw such unhappiness, and such courage, that I couldn't help crying. I'm sorry if I blew the exercise."

Phoebe swallowed hard. Her sorrow over Griffin shouldn't show so clearly. How she wished she could bury it forever.

"That's okay," she said to Alice. "I guess you were right. There's some unhappiness there. It isn't the only thing I'm feeling, though. Like you,

87

I'm feeling a sense of freedom, too. I feel like I could spread my arms and wrap them around the whole town!"

"How did you know? That's exactly right!"

Phoebe glanced over at Hugh. He was watching them with the pleased expression of a scientist whose experiment has just come out the way he hoped it would.

For the next hour Hugh took Phoebe and Alice through a whole series of mime and body movement exercises. Many of them interesting, and some were fiendishly difficult, but none carried the emotional impact of the eye-gazing exercise. It was just as well. Phoebe felt she had already had more than her recommended daily allowance of heavy emotional experiences.

She was fascinated to see how different her strengths were from Alice's. Alice moved beautifully, with precise control and natural grace. Phoebe was also fairly light and graceful on her feet. But as she followed Alice through the movement exercises, she found herself wondering if she had mistakenly put on her father's hiking boots that morning.

With the mime exercises, their positions were reversed. Phoebe found it easy to pick up and pet an imaginary cat, to stare out to sea in the teeth of a howling wind, or to carry on a silent conversation while boarding a bus and fumbling in her purse for change. Alice, on the other hand, often had to stop dead in the middle of an exercise to think through what she was going to do next. After Hugh had berated her for the third time, she broke the habit, but her brow still knotted up in thought at odd moments.

The part Phoebe enjoyed most was the vocal exercises. It was so interesting to compare what Hugh had them do to build their speaking voices with what Miss Spinelli was teaching her in her singing lessons. She was sure that Miss Spinelli wouldn't approve of some of the work; one exercise in particular. It involved standing in the middle of the stage, resting her hands lightly on her abdomen, and saying "Huh!" in as loud and deep a speaking voice as she could. Phoebe could imagine Miss Spinelli wincing.

Finally, they sat down on their folding chairs again and Hugh said, "We've made a good start today. You've both worked really well. But remember, it's just a start. I'm ready to give this as much time as it needs, and I hope you are, too."

"How much time is that?" Alice said timidly. "My parents — "

"We have our regular cast rehearsals, of course," Hugh said, almost as if she hadn't spoken, "but I expect much more from my leads. For now let's say an extra half-hour or so after each rehearsal and at least one session like this over the weekend. If we need more time, we'll take it."

"What about Art Blackstock?" Phoebe inquired. "He's playing a lead part, too."

Hugh shifted uncomfortably, as if taken aback by her question. "Later, maybe, we'll bring Art into these sessions. For now I'm working with him alone. In fact" — he glanced at his wrist — "I'm meeting him at my house in a little while. Let's set up our next session and then call it quits for the day. Can you both stay on after Monday's rehearsal? I'll have you out before six."

Both girls agreed. Hugh then offered to drive them home. As they walked out to the parking lot with him, Phoebe wondered which of them would sit in the front seat with Hugh. Maybe he'd make them arm wrestle, or draw straws. The afternoon had been rewarding for Phoebe. And she was more and more intrigued and excited at the world that was opening up to her through acting; but at the same time Hugh's exercises had left her feeling oddly like a puppet whose strings have been pulled too hard.

As it turned out, Hugh decided the issue by asking where each of them lived. Alice was the last stop, so she got the front seat. Phoebe told herself that she didn't really mind. Still, as she watched the two heads turning toward each other, carrying on a conversation that she couldn't take part in or even hear, she felt a small stab of envy. Why didn't she live a couple of blocks farther from school? It wasn't fair!

Chapter
10

Dear Bill:

I'm glad you liked *Dance Into the Sun* so much, though I think you missed a couple of things about it. It might be worth another read. Anyway, here is another poem which is *not* for publication in Imagination. I hope you'll understand why.

> There's a shy girl at Kennedy High
> With a crush on an Imaginative guy.
> Though her poems might be serious
> 'Bout him she's delirious
> She's fun, won't you give her a try?

> *Charlotte Wodehouse*

There! Cynthia thought as she folded the page and put it in the envelope, taking care that the teacher didn't observe her action. She couldn't keep from grinning wickedly. If he doesn't understand *that*, I'll just have to borrow one of Daddy's golf clubs and tap a message in Morse code on that thick skull of his!

She had put *Dance Into the Sun* in the mailbox before her first class on Monday. She had expected that he'd take a week or so to respond as he did the first time, but when she happened to pass the *Imagination* office yesterday she couldn't help looking in the box. To her astonishment, there was a note addressed to Charlotte Wodehouse.

Once again Bill said how wonderful he thought her poetry was, and once again he included a short rhymed reply to her poem. But though the reply was clever and pointed, it gave no indication that he knew her poem had been addressed to him. She didn't know whether to laugh or cry, so she figured she might as well laugh. She found an empty bench in the quad, opened her loose-leaf to a blank page, and wrote a limerick. The time for delicate poetic imagery was past.

Cynthia glanced over her shoulder at the wall clock. Seven minutes until lunch. At the thought, her stomach growled loudly. She'd missed breakfast that morning and was famished. The girl next to her heard it and giggled. Cynthia's face reddened. It grumbled again, and she shrugged helplessly.

Finally, just when she was sure she was about to faint from hunger, the bell rang. She was the fourth student out the door, and would have been first if she hadn't paused to make sure she still had the envelope.

Sasha and Phoebe were already sitting at the table in the corner. As Cynthia started toward them with her tray loaded with a cheeseburger, salad, yogurt, and Coke, Sasha noticed her and waved. The gesture warmed Cynthia. She had been sure they would welcome her, but it was nice to have it so clearly confirmed.

"Okay," Sasha was saying to Phoebe as Cynthia put her tray down, "don't listen to me. We'll ask Cynthia what she thinks. Best two out of three, all right?"

Phoebe managed to look stubborn even while she smiled.

"What I think about what?"

"The picnic on Sunday. I've been telling Pheeb — " Sasha stopped when she saw the inquiring look on Cynthia's face.

"You know about my picnic, don't you?" Sasha clapped the palm of her hand to her forehead. "Oh golly," she said, "I forgot to ask you! I remember I told your mother about it. That was last week sometime, when she stopped by the bookshop. Then I guess I must have sort of checked you off my mind. You *can* come, can't you? It's Sunday afternoon, down by the canal. Mostly people you know from Kennedy, and a few others. If you want to bring anyone, that's fine, too."

"Thanks," Cynthia said, "I'd love to come."

"Great! Now help me convince my pigheaded friend in the Cub Scout shirt that she has to come, too."

Cynthia was surprised. She knew that Sasha and Phoebe were old and close friends.

"What could keep you away from the picnic, Phoebe?" she asked.

Sasha said in a disgusted tone, "She's in a play."

"Really? That's great! The one here at school?" Phoebe nodded gloomily.

"Well, Sasha," said Cynthia, "the first performances are in a couple of weeks, aren't they? Missing a rehearsal could be a really bad move."

"It's not a rehearsal," Sasha countered. "From what Phoebe tells me, it's some sort of screwy sensitivity group."

"Actors need to be sensitive," Phoebe said defensively.

"Sure; so do dentists. That doesn't mean they have to spend their Sunday afternoons *learning* to be sensitive. Come on, Phoebe, it won't be the same without you. How often do I throw a party?"

Phoebe smiled. "As far as I can remember, about once every three years."

"So are you going to spoil such a rare event by staying away?"

"Okay, I surrender." Phoebe tossed her hands in the air. "I can't promise anything, but I'll ask Alice if there's another time we can get together. It's just the two of us, so that makes things simpler."

"Why don't you bring her along to the picnic, too?" Sasha suggested. "Then if you really feel the need, the two of you can go off and have your encounter session."

Phoebe nodded. It wasn't a bad idea. But she

didn't want to commit herself without sounding out Alice on the subject.

Cynthia glanced up from her lunch. It was all she could do to keep from swallowing her burger whole. Ted, Brenda, and Woody were approaching the table. Ted had just been describing an afternoon he and Chris had spent with Laurie Bennington and Dick Westergard at Laurie's house, and he told the story again for the benefit of Cynthia, who was the only one there who had never been to Laurie's before. Cynthia listened with a mixture of amusement and disbelief.

"The pool is nice and big," he was saying, "and the dressing rooms have their own showers, with a sauna in between them. Terrific, but nothing too outrageous. After our swim, though, we went into the house, to the *media room*." He gave the last words a villainous inflection.

Woody snorted out loud.

"I know," Ted said, "but that's what Laurie calls it, and I can see her point. It would be pretty silly just to call it the TV room. The TV screen is about six feet across and hooked up to computers, VCR's, game machines, compact disc players, and the microwave for all I know about it. Then there's the stereo, and the tape decks, and speakers in all four corners of the room, and probably a dozen other gadgets I didn't even see."

"What did you do with all that high-tech equipment?" Sasha asked.

Ted laughed. "What everybody else does on Saturday night. We made popcorn in the microwave and watched an old movie. Something called *Around the World in Eighty Days*. The plot was dumb, but the scenery was nice."

Cynthia swallowed the last spoonful of yogurt and looked at her watch. She had twelve minutes before her next class. That was plenty of time to drop the envelope off at the *Imagination* office, if she left now. She hated to leave, though; she was enjoying the company.

She began to pile her rubbish on her tray. Ted stopped in mid-sentence to give her a nod, Woody smiled, and Brenda said, "You're not leaving already, are you?"

"I have to," Cynthia explained. "I've got a couple of things to do before class."

"Well, don't forget about Sunday afternoon," Sasha said. "Do you think you'll be bringing somebody? The only reason I ask is that I want to be sure to have enough drumsticks to go around."

"Is this a picnic," Woody asked with a grin, "or a marching band rehearsal?"

Sasha stuck her tongue out at him. "You don't have to decide now," she added.

"I'm not sure," Cynthia said. "I'll let you know by Friday, if that's okay."

"Fine. We'll see you around."

As she walked through the halls, Cynthia played mental Ping-Pong with the idea of inviting Bill to the picnic. Yes, no; yes, no. She could probably manage to do it in a way that didn't sound like she was asking him for a date. She would certainly have more fun if he were there.

On the other hand, if they showed up together, maybe it would look as if they were a couple. Not that *she* minded.

At the intersection of the two halls, Cynthia stopped. The door to the *Imagination* office was propped open — that was very unusual. She approached cautiously and peeked in. Bill was there, leaning back in his editor's chair with his feet propped on his desk.

The presence in the doorway caused him to look up from his book, startled. He sat up quickly and the front legs of his chair hit the floor with a crash. "Oh, hi," he said when she saw who it was. "I won't be going straight home after school today. Mom stuffed a few bucks in my hand this morning and ordered me to the mall to buy a new swimsuit before we run into summer."

Cynthia didn't challenge his assumption that she had come by to talk about walking home together. "Why?" she asked. "Have you grown a lot since last year?"

"Not really; a little here and there. No, she's just tired of seeing me in old cut-off jeans. She'd like me to aspire to a more sophisticated poolside image."

Cynthia was only half listening. She was more concerned with the problem of delivering her new poem without him seeing her than the fine points of his summer wardrobe. The open door put the mailbox directly in his line of vision. She couldn't think of any way to do it. "Do you want to walk me to class?" she asked.

Bill shook his head. "Nope, I'm cutting the rest of the day."

"You're taking absences in three classes just to buy a bathing suit?"

"Don't be ridiculous. I've got a very special reason for hanging out here, and it doesn't have anything to do with swimsuits. Do you remember I told you about my mystery poet?"

"The girl with the phony name that you're falling in love with," said Cynthia teasingly, feeling very bold.

"That's the one. I'm expecting another message from her sometime this week, maybe today, and I'm waiting here to get it."

Cynthia blinked in alarm. What was she going to do now? She was sure the envelope with the limerick inside was glowing like a neon sign through the cover of her notebook.

She pretended not to understand. "So what? You can still go to class, can't you? Let her leave a note in the mailbox over there."

"That's just the point. She always leaves her messages in the mailbox, but this time I mean to *see* her do it. I'm going to sit here until I do, too!"

Worse and worse. "No matter how long it takes?"

"No matter how long. You don't understand, Cyn, I've *got* to find out who she is! I lie awake at night thinking about her, imagining what her face, her voice might be like. I'm going nuts!"

"And you have no idea who she is?"

"No idea at all. I don't think she's a freshman or sophomore because her poems seem too mature, but I could be wrong about that. There's such a freshness to her work."

Now that her alarm was dying down, Cynthia was beginning to enjoy herself. Talking to Bill this way made her feel like Tom Sawyer and Huckleberry Finn, attending their own funeral and hearing all the good things that were said about them.

"Why are you trying to find out who she is?" she asked innocently. "She obviously doesn't want you to. Why not just enjoy her poetry?"

"I would if I could, but it's gone way beyond that now. Don't you see, Cynthia? There's something about this girl, about her poetry, that makes me feel like we've known each other all our lives. She feels like a missing part of me."

You do know her, Cynthia wanted to shout. I am part of you. Bill had to recognize the joy in her eyes, see how thrilled she was that he shared her feelings. Cynthia was working up the nerve to confess everything when he spoke again.

"Of course, I couldn't really feel like this about somebody I already know. The strangeness and mystery are a big part of it. There's something about starting completely fresh and new with someone that lets you be more than you've been before."

Cynthia managed to keep the hurt out of her voice. "You mean old friends are like old shoes. They're really comfortable, but all the shine is gone."

"Uh-huh, that's it." Suddenly he looked at her in dismay. "I don't mean *you*, of course. You know how much your friendship means to me,

Cyn. I hope we stay friends just the way we are for the rest of our lives."

She turned away to keep him from seeing her face.

"Never mind," Bill continued. He'd stood up and moved around to sit on the front edge of the desk. "I know I'm probably being a fool. Imagine, falling in love with some girl's poetry. She'll probably turn out to be nothing like her poetry at all. It'll be your turn to laugh then."

"Leave it alone then," Cynthia advised. She pointed out the window at the stream of after-lunch traffic in the hall. "She might be any one of those girls out there. She could be anyone. She could be the janitor, or the librarian, or. . . ." Her voice trailed off.

As she hoped he would, Bill walked over to the window and gazed outward. The instant his back was turned, Cynthia slipped the envelope from her notebook into the mailbox on the open door. It stubbornly refused to go all the way in. She didn't dare continue to fumble with it. Heart pounding, she left it sticking out and tiptoed back to Bill's desk.

"You're right," he said from the window. "I know you're right, and at the same time I *can't* leave it alone. It's like an itch that has to be scratched. Once I find out who she is, maybe it'll be different. That's why I'm so determined to — *Cynthia!*"

She was expecting a reaction, but his sudden shout startled her. She jumped and her notebook clattered to the floor. Before she could say any-

100

thing, he had dashed out the door. He was gone only a few moments, just long enough for Cynthia to recover her cool.

"Of all the rotten luck," he exclaimed. "She got away from me. Did you see her?"

"Who?"

"Her! My poet!" He pointed at the envelope in the mailbox. "She must have been lurking outside, waiting until my back was turned."

He pulled the envelope from the box and ripped it open. He pulled the letter out and unfolded it. Then just as abruptly he refolded the page and stuck it in his shirt pocket. "I'll read it later, when I've calmed down," he muttered.

"It's from her, then? Chocolate Mousse?"

"Charlotte Wodehouse, and I don't think you're very funny. Yes, it's from her all right. You didn't see her at all?"

Cynthia shook her head. "I was looking at a magazine," she explained.

"Oh. And all I saw was her back as she turned a corner. She has long, dark hair, that's all I could really tell, but I think I'll know her if I see her again."

He was too involved in his own thoughts to notice the look of bewilderment on Cynthia's face, bewilderment that slowly changed to deep dismay.

Chapter
11

"Hi. I thought I'd find you out here."

Cynthia looked up, squinting against the brightness of the sky. Along with what seemed like half the student body of Kennedy High School, she was spending her Thursday study hall in the quad sitting on the grass, basking in the spring sunlight. "Oh, hi, Brenda," she said. "Sit down."

"Thanks, but I have to be somewhere." Brenda turned to go, then reconsidered. "Well, just for a minute." She sank to her knees and sat back on the heels of her black suede boots. "I wanted to tell you that I thought a lot about our conversation the other day."

"Oh?" It took Cynthia a moment to recall what conversation she meant.

"Yeah. And I finally decided that you're right. All my reasons for not writing are really just excuses. The truth is, I'm afraid that I won't have anything to say, and even if I do, I won't say it well."

"Oh, come on, what about that article of yours? Everybody loved it."

"Not everybody. Anyway, what if that was just an accident? Why not quit while I'm ahead, instead of pressing my luck and taking a chance that everyone will find out what an airhead I really am?"

Cynthia was about to speak, but Brenda continued, "Then I realized that that's all defensiveness. I should have known better, from my experiences at Garfield House. I have to take the risk of being myself, right up front, and let people react to the real me."

Cynthia opened her mouth to say something, but Brenda had only paused for breath.

"So I've decided to write some more articles for the paper," she said.

"You have?" Cynthia enthused. "Super! What about?"

"Well . . . I haven't talked to Sasha about it yet, but I thought maybe I could look at different kinds of counseling that are available to teenagers. Everything from career and college counseling to groups like Al-Anon. You know, when somebody needs help, lots of times he doesn't look for it because he doesn't even know it's around. But if he remembers reading about some organization that helps kids, even if it isn't exactly what he needs, he might decide to ask around and find out who can help with *his* problem."

"That's a *great* idea," Cynthia said emphatically. "Sasha will love it!"

"I hope so," Brenda said. "*I* think it's a good idea, but. . . ."

"You'll do what you did in that other article, won't you? Tell about some of the people involved, and their stories? That's the kind of thing that keeps people reading."

Brenda nodded. "That's what I want to do, sure. It'll take a lot of time, getting to know the people enough to write about them. But if it just helps one kid who's in trouble, it's worth it. Hey, I'm utterly late! Will you be at Sasha's picnic?" Brenda jumped to her feet. "I'll see you there if not before!"

Cynthia watched her lope across the quad, her shoulder bag banging against her back at every step. How ironic that she had managed to give Brenda such helpful advice, advice that she wasn't able to follow herself. When Brenda spoke about being up front, Cynthia had cringed inwardly. She herself was about as far from "up front" as you could be. She was out back, down below — anyplace but up front where she belonged.

She wasn't sure that anyone knew the real Cynthia Walker: not her mom or dad, not Sasha, or Brenda. Not Bill. And if so, it was her own fault. She had never dared to show herself to them.

As long as she kept herself hidden, everything could go along as it had. She and Bill could still be friends. He knew that he could always find a sympathetic listener in her. He would tell her all the ups and downs in his love life; and she'd console him and give him advice, and tell him nothing at all about her affection for him. She would settle for that rather than risk losing him altogether.

But as long as she kept herself hidden, even the little that she got from Bill wasn't really her own. By holding back, by pretending to be someone she wasn't, she was tricking Bill into being her friend.

Cynthia had signed a pen name to that first poem because she was too shy and unsure of herself to sign her own. But now that she *knew* Bill liked her poetry, what's more, liked the person behind it, she was ready to step in and claim the admiration and affection she hadn't earned honestly.

She had played games with her best friend's feelings, and Bill had always treated her with such tenderness. Like the time he invited her to the homecoming dance freshman year when he found her crying because she was sure she was the only girl without a date. Or the way he'd comforted her the night her grandfather died. Cynthia rolled over and lay on her stomach on the grass. Oh, Bill, she thought, I should have trusted you, trusted you with my true heart. You would have treated it right.

So what do I do now? Cynthia asked herself dully, wiping at a tear that had slid across her nose. She could march up to Bill and announce that she was Charlotte Wodehouse. Or break it to him gradually somehow. She was going to have to do a lot of explaining either way. Maybe Charlotte should write one last note, something like, "I'm sorry I deceived you, friend. I'll tell you everything when we finally meet"?

Cynthia buried her face in the grass and sniffled. She was hoping she looked at least a little like she was sunbathing when a knuckle tapped lightly on the back of her head and Bill's voice said, "Hey, anybody home?"

Cynthia sat up with a start. He was the last person she wanted to see at that particular moment, but she hid the fact behind a wan smile. "Hi," she said weakly.

"I've been standing here I don't know how long," he informed her, "waiting to get your attention. With your talent for not seeing people, you could earn a lot as a sales clerk at the mall."

"I'm sorry, I was thinking about something."

"Only something? I figured it had to be everything at the least. Never mind, I have the most incredible news to tell you." He dropped his books and sat down next to her.

Not as amazing as the news I have to tell you, Cynthia thought. But all she said was, "Oh? What?"

He grinned triumphantly at her. "I know who Charlotte Wodehouse is! What do you have to say about that?"

"Really?" she said cautiously. "How did you find out?"

"That's the strange part. I was looking at one of her poems and at the way she signed her name, and suddenly instead of seeing the whole

106

name I saw only the initials. You know, sometimes people who choose false names keep their real initials, even if they don't notice they're doing it." He looked at her expectantly.

Cynthia blinked. He knew who she was. She studied his face surreptitiously. He seemed to be taking it very well. She didn't see any sign of resentment. If anything, he seemed excited and proud. She felt her face flush with warmth now that the moment of revelation had arrived.

"That was pretty smart," she said.

"Yes, it was, wasn't it?" There was a touch of complacency in his voice.

"I didn't even realize — " she began, but he interrupted her.

"Of course, there must be lots of girls with those initials," he said. "It wouldn't have helped me that much if I hadn't caught a glimpse of her yesterday afternoon."

"A glimpse — !"

"That long, dark hair — I recognized it when I walked by her just now. I asked somebody who she was, and I found out she's a sophomore named Carol Winstanley. Get it? *C. W.* That proves it."

Cynthia couldn't speak. She knew that if she tried she would croak like a frog. When she swallowed, a bitter taste forced itself up into her throat.

"Don't look now," he continued, "but that's her sitting with the two guys on the bench by the tree. She's the one in the blue-and-yellow

107

Hawaiian shirt. She has a very sensitive face, doesn't she?"

Cynthia looked around, as nonchalantly as she could, and easily spotted the girl he meant. The shirt was hard to overlook. She didn't look at all that sensitive to Cynthia. Granted, she was pretty, but just ordinary pretty. She did have a nice smile and she was putting it to good use while she chatted with her two admirers.

"She reminds me of Ophelia, in *Hamlet*," Bill announced.

More like Scarlett O'Hara in *Gone with the Wind*, Cynthia thought, not too charitably.

Bill raved on. "She looks so fresh, so tender."

"Like asparagus," Cynthia said, but she had the sense to say it too softly for him to hear. The two sat and watched the girl in question as she defended herself in a playful tickling match.

"If only I could talk to her, I know we'd have so much in common. It's as if we've known each other forever. Not just in this lifetime, but in many lifetimes."

"It shouldn't be hard to talk to someone you've known that long. Just walk over and say, 'Hi there, haven't seen you around since 1743. How's everything been?' "

"Now just stop that, Cyn. This may seem funny to you, but it's a serious matter for me. I'm telling you, I love that girl's soul!"

"You've never even met her!"

"I've met her soul and her mind, in her poetry. What else matters?"

"You don't even know that she's the one who

wrote those poems," she said, as gently and per-
suasively as she could. "Don't jump blindly into
something like this. You could be making a big
mistake."

"But I do know she's the one. Her initials — "

" — could be a coincidence. You don't
know — "

"All I have to do is look at her to know!"

Cynthia sighed and fell silent. Bill seemed
determined to talk himself into an infatuation
with the girl on the bench. She could stop him by
telling him the truth, right this minute. And the
truth might embarrass him so deeply that he
would resent her for the rest of his life. He might
not even believe her, though she could prove it
if she had to — and if he would listen.

If she had never picked that stupid name. . . .
Maybe losing Bill to Carol Whosits was exactly
what she deserved for not being more open with
him in the first place. But C. W. — Bill might
have taken a closer look at that poetic soul. His
old friend Cynthia Walker had been looking
back at him the whole time.

Cynthia picked at the grass while Bill continued to study Carol for further signs of sensitivity. She didn't want to see him hurt or
humiliated, and it was sure to happen if he pur-
sued this. She had set Bill on the wrong path and
now she had to set him right. It might cost her
his friendship, but it was still her duty.

"Bill," she began, "suppose she really is your
mystery poet. Why did she use a phony name?
To keep her identity a secret, right? Don't you

think you ought to respect that, and wait for her to tell you who she is? If she wants you to know, she *will* tell you somehow. And if she doesn't, that's her choice."

"You're right, Cyn, I know you are. But don't you see: I *can't* wait, not now that I know. Listen, maybe you could get to know her, and then introduce me. I'd feel weird just walking over and saying hello. What do you say?"

Cynthia's feelings of guilt were suddenly submerged by a wave of anger. It was hard enough to have to listen to him talking about that girl. She certainly wasn't going to play matchmaker! "No, I couldn't," she said firmly. "According to you, the two of you have been exchanging passionate poems for the last couple of weeks. Why do you need to be introduced? She knows who you are."

She knew she was being unfair. But Bill refused to listen to her. Let him find out the hard way how wrong he was.

He had flushed. "You're not being very understanding, Cynthia. I don't know why, but she won't look at me. She acts like she doesn't know me from Adam. Maybe she only knows my name and not what I look like. I can't just —" Bill broke off as the girl and her two friends stood up and started to walk away. "Hey, I'll catch you later," he said to Cynthia. Without waiting for a response, he started off after them. When they left the quad and passed out of sight, he was only a few feet behind them.

Cynthia's thoughts spun and tumbled like socks

110

in a dryer. She wanted to protect Bill, but she wanted to protect herself, too. Bill had said he was in love with the mind and soul of his mystery poet, but that wasn't a mind and soul he had just followed across the quad. It was a real live sophomore with the initials C.W. By the time he discovered that she wasn't his poet, he might not care about poetry anymore. He might have taken up tickling.

She clutched a fistful of grass and tossed it into the air. A good portion of it got caught by the breeze and was blown back into her face. Cynthia sneezed. What a mess. All she had meant to do was to express her feelings to Bill, her love as well as her fears and doubts, without risking too much. As it turned out, she had risked *everything* — and it was starting to look as if she'd lost.

Chapter
12

Phoebe was following Miss Spinelli down the hall of her house to the studio when the telephone rang. "Why don't you go on in," her voice teacher said. "I won't be a moment."

The double doors were glass-paned, but sheer curtains preserved the feeling of privacy. Phoebe put her music book down on the long oak table and looked around.

Every detail proclaimed that this was a workroom. On the walls were framed concert posters, old sheet music covers, and engravings of singers, musicians, and instruments. An old stoneware crock in the corner held an assortment of recorders, penny whistles, and bamboo flutes. One tall glass-fronted bookcase contained dictionaries, reference works, and music journals, while two others were filled with scores of operas and oratorios, collections of lieder, and volumes of show tunes and popular songs. The old ebony Steinway grand piano in the center of the room gleamed in the light from an amber glass chandelier.

Phoebe let the peace of the room quiet her mind. Too much had been happening too quickly in her life these days; she felt like she was getting lost in the shuffle.

"I'm sorry," Miss Spinelli said as she bustled into the room. "Shall we begin?" She stood behind the piano and looked at Phoebe. "Hmm . . . your body seems a little tense, dear, a little rigid. Before we get into our vocal exercises, let's try to loosen up, shall we?"

She led Phoebe through a short series of movements that began with shrugging her shoulders and ended with bending double at the waist and letting her head and arms dangle loosely toward the floor. "Oh yes, much better," she commented when Phoebe straightened up again. "When we are tense, the notes have less room to come out. Our vocal passages become distorted, and that distorts the purity of the sound."

"Now — " She played a note on the piano and sang an easy scale, five notes up and four back down. Phoebe sang it back to her, then listened as she played the same scale a tone higher. Each time, after Phoebe copied her, she moved the scale up a step. Very soon they reached Phoebe's upper range and the scales were not so easy anymore. Just at the point that Phoebe was sure her voice was going to crack, Miss Spinelli paused and said, "Very good. Were you aware that you went two notes higher just now than you did last week?"

Phoebe shook her head.

"Your natural range is wider than you have ever allowed yourself to use. That's true of many people. I can't think of anyone who's studied with me who didn't gain a greater range sooner or later. It's partly a matter of working up to your limits by easy stages, and partly a matter of having the confidence that the notes are there." They began another exercise.

After fifteen minutes or so of vocal work, Phoebe felt that she was as ready to sing as she was going to get that afternoon. Miss Spinelli seemed to share that feeling. As Phoebe finished a long, rather elaborate scale, she opened her notebook and said, "What have you been working on this week? Oh yes, I gave you an Elizabethan lute song; and you found a piece by Jacques Brel. Let's look at the lute song first."

Phoebe found the music, set it on the stand, and got ready to sing.

"No, no," Miss Spinelli called, "you are putting too much effort into preparing. You are about to sing, not lift a heavy suitcase! Try to relax."

Phoebe used Hugh's technique to find her tension spots and tell them to go away. It seemed to work.

"Good. And — "

Phoebe began to sing. The piano started and then fell silent. Phoebe stopped.

"The notes are right, dear, but did you hear yourself sing *smi-hi-hi-hi-hiles*? Think of your scales. Let's start again, and remember to move smoothly and easily from note to note."

114

They worked on the lute song for twenty minutes. Phoebe had never dreamed that singing involved so much problem solving and memorization of details. It had always been something she simply *did*. But under Miss Spinelli's guidance, she was beginning to learn *how* to do it. The last time they ran through the song, she could not only hear the improvement but notice places that still needed work.

"That's coming along," her teacher said. The praise made Phoebe glow with pleasure. The whole day seemed a little brighter because she was singing well.

"Now, let me see," Miss Spinelli continued, searching through a stack of music books on the table next to the piano. "Where did I put that volume of Brel? Here we are." She opened the book and propped it on the music rack, then looked expectantly at Phoebe.

The song was called "If We Only Have Love." Phoebe had first chosen to work on it because she thought both the melody and the lyrics were wonderful. She still did. Now that she faced the prospect of singing it for Miss Spinelli, however, she realized that choosing it had been a mistake. The song had too many painful associations for her.

Griffin had first introduced her to the songs of Jacques Brel, and he had singled this one out as his own favorite. She could still hear him singing it and urging her to make up a harmony line on the spot.

"Phoebe? Are you ready?"

She nodded, looked down at the music, and opened her mouth. But instead of starting to sing, she said, "I'm sorry, Miss Spinelli. I don't think I can sing this song."

"Oh? Technically it shouldn't give you any difficulties. The range is just right." She gave Phoebe a shrewd yet sympathetic look. "But perhaps the difficulty is not technical. Very well, dear. Let me see: Do you know any of the songs of Leonard Cohen? No? He was very popular some years ago. Here's one I think you'll like. I'll play it through once for you."

As she played, Phoebe studied the music. The song was called "Suzanne," and the words were strangely evocative. Somehow they seemed to fit perfectly with her mood. The song was oddly familiar, as if she'd heard it before. She felt as if she could almost sing it now, if only she could somehow sneak past the part of her mind that was sure she didn't know it.

"That's beautiful," she sighed when the piano fell silent.

"Do you want to try it? We have just enough time before my next student is due."

"No, I. . . ." Phoebe looked at her watch. Her lesson had run over as it was. "I'll take this home and work on it this week, if that's okay."

Phoebe waved good-bye to Miss Spinelli and started down the sidewalk. She hesitated and looked at her watch again. She had a private session with Hugh at the Little Theater in thirty-five minutes. She didn't have time to go home before her rehearsal, but if she went straight to

116

school she would be nearly half an hour early.

A door slammed behind her. She turned and saw Michael Rifkin coming down the steps. He waved and cut across the lawn toward her.

"Michael. Hi," Phoebe said with a smile. "How's the music coming for the play? I haven't seen you at any rehearsals."

"No, I'm doing most of the composing here at home," Michael said.

"Isn't Hugh terrific?" Phoebe asked. "I have learned *so much* working with him, I can't even begin to tell you. I just hate the fact that I didn't meet him until now, when he's about to graduate. My rehearsals with him are literally the high point of my day." Phoebe looked at her watch. "As a matter of fact, I have to go off to one now."

"Oh? Are you walking? I'll keep you company, if you don't mind. I'm going that way."

Of course she didn't mind Michael's company; in fact she welcomed it. As they neared the corner, she said, "I didn't know you were a composer, as well as a cellist."

He laughed. "I've written some things, but I'm not sure I'd call myself a composer. Writing's not such a big deal. Anybody who's learned the language can write music. The real trick is to write *good* music."

"I bet yours is very good." Phoebe was really impressed. "You have such a wonderful musical background."

He gave another laugh. "If you mean there's music going on in my house all the time, you're right. But you'd be surprised how hard that

117

makes it to think. I wouldn't mind a solid week or two of complete silence — except for the noise *I* make, of course."

Phoebe joined his laughter. How nice it was to talk to someone who took what he did seriously but still managed to stay lighthearted about it. When she'd talked with Griffin, she'd gotten the feeling that he felt the entire future of the human race somehow rested on the achievements of modern drama. She was starting to realize how important it was to strike a balance.

For the next few blocks she and Michael talked easily about friends they had in common. As they came in sight of the campus, Phoebe expected him to say good-bye to her and go on his way. Instead, he said, "You know, I really should make the time to come to more of Hugh's rehearsals. The script doesn't give me enough of a feel for the play to write really effective music. Why don't I come along with you now? I can always do my errand afterward."

Phoebe began to stumble through an explanation that this rehearsal was going to be just Hugh and her. The look Michael gave her as she spoke made her face turn as red as her hair. She could tell what was going through his mind. He thought that she had a thing going with Hugh.

What embarrassed her most was that she wasn't sure he would be entirely wrong. She found Hugh more fascinating with every encounter. Certainly she was looking forward to this rehearsal, her first with him alone, with unusual excitement, and unusual nervousness. The thought of all that passionate intelligence, all that magnetism, focused entirely on her made Phoebe tingle from head to toe. The persistent feeling that Hugh was somehow dangerous to her only drew her in deeper and increased her excitement.

"Hey, that's cool," Michael said when her explanation dribbled to a close. "I'll catch a full rehearsal next week. No problem. You'd better take off now; you don't want to be late. Tell Hugh I said hello and that I'll be in touch, will you?"

"Sure," she replied gratefully.

The door to the theater stood ajar. Phoebe slipped into the gloom that had become so familiar, then stopped. Inside the auditorium, someone was speaking lines from the play. She couldn't mistake that voice. What was Alice doing here? This was *Phoebe's* rehearsal, her special time with Hugh!

Maybe Hugh had set an earlier appointment with Alice and they hadn't finished yet. Phoebe stepped back outside into the light to check her watch. She was right on time. The proper thing to do, then, was to let them know that she was here. As soon as they wrapped up whatever they were doing, *she* could take the stage.

She knew she had a perfect right to be there, but she still felt like an intruder as she walked down the aisle. Hugh was onstage, standing next to Alice, one hand on her shoulder. He was talking to her in an undertone. Alice's face as she listened spelled out in banner headlines that she had a massive crush on him. Phoebe couldn't decide if she was amused or disgusted. Why couldn't Alice control herself, at least until after the play was over!

They still hadn't noticed her. "Hello," she called loudly. Alice jumped away from Hugh.

"Hi, Phoebe," Hugh said evenly.

"Hello," said Alice. Her tone and expression translated her greeting into "What are you doing here?"

Phoebe chose to answer the unspoken question. "Well," she said breezily, "I'm ready to rehearse. Have you guys finished yet?"

"Finished?" Alice repeated. "We just started!"

Hugh stepped forward to the apron. "Ah . . . it's partly my fault, I'm afraid. I wanted to have individual sessions with each of you. But when we set our schedule, I wrote both of you in at this time."

Partly your fault, thought Phoebe, it's *all* your fault. But even while thinking that, she aimed her anger at Alice, though she knew how irrational that was.

"I'll go away and come back in an hour," she said tersely.

"No need for that," Hugh replied. "I can work with the two of you just as well. After all, you are playing against each other, aren't you?"

As she mounted the stairs to the stage, Phoebe thought to herself that Hugh's words were truer than he realized. As if he read her mind, the director nodded in satisfaction.

Chapter
13

Cynthia braked to a stop at the head of the path. This was her first view of the new picnic area, and part of her was enjoying the beautiful spot. The rest was quailing at the sight of fifteen or twenty kids standing around in little groups near the canal bank. The table closest to Cynthia was piled high with grocery bags, cardboard boxes, and coolers.

It had to be Sasha's picnic. She thought she could even see Sasha. But this was not exactly what she had expected. When her mother had asked how many people to fix fruit salad for, Cynthia had guessed eight. To her eye, it looked as if half of Kennedy High were there.

Cynthia couldn't wheel around and go back home, not with two big containers of fruit salad strapped to the back of her bike. Besides, Sasha had seen her and was waving. She took a deep breath, pushed off, and coasted down the path toward the party.

Sasha came over as she was parking her bike. "Isn't this amazing?" she said. "We may end up taking over the whole picnic area. I was up until three baking granola cookies, and I'm still not sure I made enough."

"When you say you're inviting a few friends, you don't mess around," Cynthia joked.

"Me? I didn't ask half the people here. No, I told everybody to bring a friend or two if they wanted, and this is the result. By the way, did you ask anybody?" Sasha looked around Cynthia as though she might have a friend strapped to her bike, alongside the fruit salad.

"No, I didn't." She had meant to ask Bill, but he'd been so busy jabbering about his "discovery" of Charlotte Wodehouse that she hadn't had a chance. And she hadn't seen him since he rushed off after the girl he was sure was his poet.

"Oh, that's okay," Sasha said, helping her with the containers of fruit. "You'll find lots of people you know. Come on, I'd like you to meet my friend Wes."

Sasha led Cynthia toward a little clump of people dominated by a tall, good-looking boy in a uniform. "Wes is at Leesburg Academy," Sasha confided. "We had a real time of it, getting my mom and dad to accept this relationship. They're not very hot on the military, you see, and he wants to be a career Navy pilot."

Cynthia looked grave as she pondered the complexities of Sasha's situation. Then Wes,

Sasha, and the Navy were driven from her mind. The girl standing next to Wes was Carol Winstanley. What was she doing here?

"Cynthia, this is Wes," Sasha was saying. "Don't let all the braid and shiny buttons scare you; he's really a pushover." She slipped her arm into his and smiled up at him. "Oh, and do you know Carol? She's one of our up-and-coming reporters at *The Red and the Gold*. I've been trying to talk Cynthia into writing for us," she told Carol, who couldn't have looked less interested.

Wes greeted Cynthia and they began a conversation about life at Leesburg. Wes's manner was serious, but friendly. Cynthia, however, couldn't help being more interested in watching dark-haired Carol Winstanley, who was yawning in ill-disguised boredom. She *would* have to turn out to be a writer! When Bill found that out, he'd be sure to take that as conclusive evidence.

Phoebe took her time getting to the picnic, cutting across town to meet the canal about a mile upstream, then strolling along the old towpath. Now and then she stopped to skip a stone across the water. She was looking forward to seeing her friends, but she also needed some time alone to think over what had happened at the rehearsal with Hugh and Alice.

They had begun as they always did, with a series of sensitivity and mime exercises. This time, though, instead of bringing them closer to each other, the exercises seemed designed to drive them farther apart. She had still been upset about losing her private time with Hugh, and Alice seemed just as annoyed. And Hugh, who was usually so reserved with both of them, had been positively electric. He seemed to send out sparks, painful, goading sparks. At one point he lost his temper and raised his voice at Alice. When she burst into tears, Phoebe watched her with detachment. She was horrified to find that she was almost glad at Alice's hurt.

What bothered Phoebe most was her instinctive awareness that Hugh was attracted to her. But every time they began to feel close he jumped back. She didn't know if she was pushing him away or he her. She only knew it was becoming impossible for her to concentrate on her acting. She had to confront him as soon as she could get a moment alone with him, before her distraction ruined the entire production.

This turned out to be very hard. After the rehearsal, she hung around waiting for him, but then Alice hung around waiting for *her*. When she told Alice to go on without her, Hugh overheard and suggested that he give both of them a ride. She recalled that Alice ordinarily got out last and said she was going to her voice teacher's in order to be the one left alone with Hugh. Then Alice claimed that she had to go to the mall rather than home, and suggested that he drop Phoebe off on the way. Phoebe was finally reduced to saying that she just remembered her singing lesson was cancelled but she needed fresh air and would love a long ride in his convertible. Hugh was willing, but Alice did not look pleased.

The silence was thick all the way to the mall, and it did not disperse even after Alice left the car. They had taken a spin and were turning onto Phoebe's block before she found the nerve to say, "I'm worried about the way things are going."

"What things, Phoebe?"

"I don't know . . . the play, you and me, you and Alice, *me* and Alice. . . ."

He chuckled. "That's a pretty complete list."

"Don't patronize me, Hugh," she said sharply.

He pulled up at the curb. "I feel it, too," he said, "but I was hoping you wouldn't. I should have known that you were too sensitive, too aware, for it to slip past you." He paused and looked down at his hands. "This is just between us, Phoebe. The fact is, Alice has let herself develop a sort of crush on me. She's very young in some ways. I've tried to tell her, as gently as I could, that I feel close to her, but only as a friend, but she won't listen. She's gotten it in her head that you are coming between her and me."

"That's ridiculous!"

"Of course it is, but that's what she believes. So even though I want to get to know you better, I don't dare do anything about it. Not until after we've finished our run. I can't take the chance of Alice getting so upset that she performs badly, or even leaves the cast."

"I see," Phoebe said. "But why don't I simply tell her that you and I aren't interested in each other that way? That we're colleagues who like and respect each other, but nothing more?"

He shook his head. "I'm afraid it wouldn't work. By speaking to her, you would confirm her suspicions that we're getting together behind her back and talking about her. No, the only thing we can do is keep our distance from each other. It's very hard for me" — Hugh's voice caught — "but we owe it to each other, to the other cast members, and to the play itself." He let out the clutch and crept down the block to her driveway. "I'd better go," he said. "I'll see you on Monday, and I'll think about you every moment until then."

He picked up her hand and gently kissed her palm.

"Hugh — " she said.

"No, Phoebe. Not now."

A moment later she was standing in her yard, watching his car disappear around the corner.

The first person Phoebe saw when she arrived at the picnic area was Woody. He'd outdone himself. In honor of the warm weather, he was wearing surfing shorts and a sleeveless shirt, but he had refused to abandon his red suspenders. The combination made such an odd picture that Phoebe had to smile.

"Hey, Pheeb-a-rebop," he said, "why so pale and quiet? Come cavort with the rest of us."

"Thanks very much," she replied, "but I can cavort just fine right where I am. Is Kim here?"

"She'll be along later. She had to help her mother with a last-minute catering job."

"I'm surprised you're not helping, too."

"I offered, but Mrs. Barrie said I take up too much room in the kitchen. The real reason," he confided with a grin, "is that I'm too theatrically oriented. You know: Who cares how it tastes as long as it looks okay from the audience!"

"How are the sets for *Adam* coming?" Phoebe asked. She knew that he had been spending almost every evening working at the Little Theater.

"Done long since," he replied. "These supermodern plays are a cinch. You don't have to bust yourself making wood and canvas look like a living room, or a backyard, or the castle walls of Elsinore. All you need is three or four platforms of different heights, a couple of flats painted in solid colors, and a scrim curtain.

"No," he added, after pulling at his can of soda, "the lighting is what's giving me fits. Hugh knows exactly what he wants, for sure, but he's not too swift about what's possible."

Phoebe stiffened slightly, then caught herself. Woody was certainly entitled to have his own opinion about Hugh's methods.

"You've been working pretty hard yourself, haven't you?" he said. "I've been watching, and I can see the changes. You'll give a super performance."

"Do you think so? I still don't feel that I know what I'm doing. If it weren't for Hugh, I'd be completely lost."

"Umph. That reminds me." Woody stopped, as if unsure how to continue. "I couldn't help noticing what's been going on."

"Going on?" she said in an ominous voice. "I

127

don't know what you're referring to."

"Well . . . Hugh can be a very charismatic fellow, but he doesn't always notice the effect he's having on people. On girl people. I've seen it happen before, so when you and Alice started getting hung up on him, I picked right up on it. Maybe you think this is none of my business — "

"That's exactly right, it's none of your business."

" — but you're an old friend, and I don't want to see you get hurt. You've had more than your share of that already this year."

"Listen here, Woodrow Webster," Phoebe said icily, "I have two things to say to you. The first is that I am not 'hung up' on Hugh Cromwell. I have tremendous respect and admiration for his talent and sensitivity. Anyone who has worked with him and who isn't hopelessly prejudiced would be bound to. The second thing I have to say is this: Kindly butt out!"

She spun on her heel and stalked away in a rage. Woody had no right to spy on her and pass judgment on her conduct, nor to be so down on Hugh. Woody was usually one of the most tolerant people she knew. What was the cause of his sudden, irrational hostility?

Then it came to her. Woody and Hugh were both interested in theater, and the conclusion was obvious: Woody was jealous. He was jealous of Hugh's talent and success. Perhaps he was jealous of her regard for Hugh, too. After all, until she met Hugh, she had always considered Woody her resident expert on everything dramatic. And hadn't he had a long-standing romantic interest in her that didn't ease up until he hooked up with Kim? It was natural for Woody to think there was something romantic between her and Hugh and to resent it.

Now that she had an explanation for his behavior, Phoebe's anger faded. It must be very hard for Woody to observe Hugh's success from behind the scenes. She could sympathize with that. She would feel the same way if Alice took the whole spotlight and left her in shadow.

As if her thought was a magical summons, Alice appeared at the top of the bank and came down the path toward the party. Phoebe's eyes narrowed. Then she reminded herself that she and Alice were friends as well as colleagues. As long as Hugh didn't show up as well, maybe she would be able to keep that fact in mind.

Cynthia was enjoying herself. She was meeting more of her classmates in one afternoon than she usually met in a semester. She was joking with Janie Barstow and Henry Braverman about staging a fashion show for pets, when she saw Bill arrive. Her first impulse was to rush over and say hi, but she decided to wait for him to make a move. He seemed ill at ease. Instead of talking to his friends from school, he stayed on the outskirts of the party, just looking around.

His eyes met Cynthia's. Instead of a smile of recognition, he gave her an imploring look. She went across to see what was wrong.

"Listen, Cyn," he said without a greeting, "if

anybody asks, can I say I'm your guest?"

"Why . . . sure, I guess so. I meant to ask you, but — " A look of amazement crossed her face. "Bill, are you crashing this party?"

"Yeah, I guess I am."

"But you never do things like that! You're too — too honorable!"

"Yeah, well this is a special occasion." Bill was glancing around them distractedly.

"Oh? Why?" She was beginning to suspect the answer.

"Look, never mind the third degree," he flared. "Just forget I asked." His gaze fixed itself on a point over Cynthia's right shoulder. She didn't really need to look, but she looked anyway. Carol Winstanley was standing on the opposite edge of the crowd.

"Bill — " she began hopelessly. But he didn't even hear her. After a couple of moments, she walked away.

Nearby, Peter Lacey and Monica Ford were engaged in a heated conversation with a couple of their friends. Peter was trying to convince them all that Bruce Springsteen was the modern equivalent of Bach or Beethoven. She listened in for a while, and even threw in a few thoughts of her own, but her mind was not really on the topic.

She glanced over at Bill several times. Each time was the same. He was standing by himself, looking fixedly at Carol, who seemed unaware of his existence.

Chapter
14

Phoebe leaned against the open stage door and stared out at the rain. It had started in the middle of sixth period with a thunderclap that rattled the windows. The downpour that followed set the gutters awash and turned the quad into a shallow pond. By now, however, it had settled into a steady fall that seemed prepared to continue for a week or two.

The afternoon's rehearsal had been affected by the weather. Not only the drumming on the roof, which sometimes drowned out the actors' voices, but the dampness, which brought peculiar musty smells up from the cellar of the old chapel. Art set everybody on edge by suggesting that there were undiscovered vaults and catacombs down there, filled with mummified corpses. Hugh told him to put less imagination into his random remarks and more into his acting.

At the end of the rehearsal, Hugh had taken Phoebe aside. She was very aware of Alice watching them. "Can you stay after the others leave?" he said. "I've been thinking about what you said. You're right, I need to work individually with the principals, and that means you. It's been unprofessional of me to let personal considerations keep me from doing it."

He seemed so contrite that Phoebe had a strong urge to comfort him. If Alice hadn't been standing a few feet away, she might have put an arm around him. She certainly would have patted his shoulder. As it was, she limited herself to saying, "Of course I'll stay, Hugh." But her tone of voice said much more than her words.

His eyes told her that he understood. "I have to go over some of the lighting cues with Fred, who'll be running the board," he explained. "It shouldn't take more than ten minutes, though. Then we'll have the place to ourselves."

The ten minutes had stretched out to fifteen, then twenty, before Hugh came hurrying over. "Sorry, love," he said. "Sometimes these techies deliberately complicate things, just to prove to you how essential they are."

She stretched her arm out the door and let the raindrops fall on her palm. "It's okay. Is everyone gone?"

"Yes, finally. The worst part of the theater is that there are always so many people hanging around. Let's go onstage." He took her wet hand and led her down the narrow corridor between the back of the set and the lines of ropes that controlled the curtains.

"I don't know why I haven't told you how gifted I think you are," he said suddenly.

"Really?" Phoebe felt both thrilled and wary. Hugh's hand was very warm on hers. "In what way?"

He turned to face her. "How can I express it? You have such a fine intuitive grasp of character, such a depth of sympathy for what the role implies. Watching you has shown me a great deal I never realized about my play. Helen is not my creation anymore, she is *ours*."

"It's a wonderful role," she murmured. "I don't even begin to understand what all her speeches mean."

"There's a lot of symbolism in them," he explained. "Then there's your voice. Most of the kids in the cast have no idea how to use their voices. They speak the same way they do every day, and when I tell them they can't be heard from the audience, they start shouting. Or worse, they ham it up like old-time vaudeville actors."

Phoebe chuckled.

"But you, Phoebe, you use your voice like an instrument. Your placement and projection are marvelous. And you put so much character into your voice! When you speak, you aren't some high-school girl reading a line. I close my eyes, and I hear Helen, speaking from her life."

Phoebe was beginning to feel the way she felt two-thirds of the way through a banana split, aware that she had had enough, but still greedy for more.

Hugh was still speaking. "The only thing I find disappointing in you, Phoebe, is your ability to take direction. You don't always listen." This was so much on target that she couldn't help blushing. She preferred hearing compliments.

"I get distracted," she said.

"Of course. We all do. But it's more than that. I often sense a resistance, a reluctance to take direction. Such resistance often goes with talent; I know that. But even a talent like yours needs someone who can stand outside, to watch and correct. That's what the director is for. I want to help you. But I can't bring out your full ability unless you trust me."

"Hugh! Of course I trust you!"

He placed a hand on each of her shoulders and looked deep into her eyes. "You think you trust me, but on a deeper level you are holding back. I need to have your total, complete confidence. There are some exercises for building trust. Are you willing to try them?"

"Of course I am," she said. "What do I do?"

The first exercise sounded simple. He was going to stand behind her. She was to let herself fall straight back, and he would catch her. The important thing was to *let* herself fall, to stay relaxed, to believe that he would keep her from being hurt.

This turned out to be very difficult The first couple of times were all right. His arms caught her before she was completely aware of falling, but the third time he moved farther back. She fell past the point where she expected to be caught, and panic seized her. She was tensing for the impact when she felt his hands under her arms, taking her weight and lowering it gently to the floor. The next time she had trouble letting herself fall at all, but she continued to work on it. Eventually she managed a fall with a completely relaxed body.

"That's super," said Hugh. "You can feel the difference, can't you?"

What she felt was emotional exhaustion. She would never have thought that trusting someone was so much work. But when he asked if she was ready for another exercise, Phoebe nodded.

"I want you to close your eyes now, and keep them closed," he instructed. She did as she was told. "Now I'm going to take your hand and lead you around the theater. All I want you to do is follow, eyes closed. Don't try to figure out where we are or what is to come, just trust my lead. Are you ready?"

For the first few steps Phoebe felt like giggling. It was sort of like blindman's buff. But gradually Hugh's intensity began to affect her. She knew by the sounds and smells that they were going backstage, but she pushed thoughts of her surroundings aside and concentrated on the self-assuredness of Hugh's grasp. She wanted to do the exercise right, to please him.

"Five steps down," he warned. "Here's the first one."

She nearly stumbled, but his arm supported

her. They walked up an aisle, then along a row of seats and down the other aisle. Keeping her eyes closed was a strain, but it seemed to sharpen her other senses. Her hearing was especially keen. She heard each footstep and its faint echo from the wall, and the distant creak of the front door, even through the pattering of the rain.

"Five steps up now. One . . . two. . . ."

They were back on stage. When Hugh let go of her hand, Phoebe congratulated herself on doing the exercise so easily. She was about to open her eyes when he wrapped his arms around her and started to kiss her. Startled, she pulled back, but he tightened his grip.

Phoebe's heart pounded. Her thoughts raced through her mind. Hugh had told her to trust him completely and follow where he led, and she had agreed, but this certainly wasn't the sort of exercise she had imagined.

If he was acting, he was doing a great job of it. His lips were painfully hard against hers. It was unnerving but exciting to imagine that she really was completely in his power. Dangerously exciting.

Suddenly, the kiss had gone on long enough. Phoebe pulled her head back and began to push at him, just as one of his hands slipped down to her waist. Sliding out of his grasp, she stepped away.

Hugh was having trouble catching his breath, but he managed to say, "That was super, Phoebe. You're getting much better at trusting. But I think you still need more practice."

He reached out, but she moved off and watched him warily. Her cheeks were flushed. "Thanks," she said, "but I guess it'll have to wait. I'd better get home. My mom didn't know I'd be this long; she might worry."

"We'll have another private session after rehearsal tomorrow — no, I mean Wednesday. Warn your mother that you'll be late. You won't forget?"

She shook her head and turned to go. As she did, she noticed a figure in the shadows at the rear of the auditorium. Michael Rifkin stepped forward into the light.

"Hugh?" he called. "You said you wanted to talk to me about the music?"

"Oh," said Hugh, flustered. "Right, Mike. I'm sorry, I forgot you were coming by. Phoebe," he added in an undertone, "I'll see you tomorrow. Don't forget what you've learned about trusting. Nothing is more important."

She couldn't speak. She turned and ran down the steps. Michael gave her an expressionless nod as she passed him in the aisle.

A light rain was still falling. Too late, Phoebe recalled that her umbrella was somewhere backstage. There was no way she was going back for it. She turned up the collar of her jacket and walked out into the damp, chilly evening.

Cynthia was enjoying the rain. It suited her gray, soggy mood. She stood just outside the main entrance at Kennedy, letting the drizzle soak her fluffy brown hair. If the day had been bright and sunny, she would have taken it as a personal offense. She was only a little bit sorry she was wishing a gloomy day on the whole town.

Bill's behavior at the picnic had ruined yesterday, and today as well. No, Cynthia corrected herself, I have to be fair. *My* behavior ruined yesterday. And today, and probably tomorrow. Her mind was flooded with "if onlys." The only thing that was a certainty was how completely she had complicated everything beyond any hope of redemption.

If she had only confessed to Bill in the first place that she was Charlotte Wodehouse; if she had kept her poems where they belonged, in her desk drawer. . . . She might have discovered that Bill cared for her. She might still have her old friend to talk to and laugh with. Instead there was a stranger in that friend's place, mooning over some other girl.

A two-hundred-pound six-footer in a soaking wet slicker rushed up the steps and slammed into her, knocking her books out of her arms. "Sorry," Cynthia said, kneeling hastily to get her notepad out of range of his size-twelve sneakers.

"Watch where you're going next time," her assailant growled.

Cynthia took this as a hint to start down the steps and move toward safer waters. She should really just go home. She could make some hot chocolate and settle down with her homework. What fun.

She glanced up to see Phoebe Hall coming down the sidewalk toward her. Apparently

Phoebe was someone else who enjoyed the rain. Not only was she bareheaded like Cynthia, but she hadn't even worn a coat.

As they drew closer, Cynthia was about to make some funny-dumb remark like, "Nice day for ducks, isn't it?" Then she noticed that Phoebe's cheeks were much wetter than the light rain could explain. "Hey, are you all right?" she said, putting a hand on Phoebe's arm.

Phoebe smiled faintly. "I'm fine," she said. "No, I'm not, either. The truth is, I'm rotten."

"Really? So am I. Do you want to start a club?"

Phoebe laughed through her tears. She had just spent the afternoon trying to learn to trust Hugh, and possibly — she still wasn't sure — making a complete fool of herself in the process. But something about Cynthia made her feel that here was someone she *could* trust, without any effort at all.

"Maybe we should," she said. She looked around as if surprised to see where she was. "Hey, it's still raining. And I'm all wet!"

Cynthia grinned. "Uh-huh. Would you like to come over to my house for cocoa and a towel? I think there's a new bag of Oreos, too."

"That's the best idea I've heard all day," Phoebe said gratefully.

Chapter
15

By the time Phoebe left Cynthia's house, the rain had stopped. She jogged most of the way home, partly to work off her tension and partly because she was late. She arrived just as her parents and little brother were sitting down to supper. She quickly changed out of her damp clothes and joined them.

Dinner was homemade chicken pot pie. It was one of her mother's specialties, and a great favorite of Phoebe's; but she had difficulty finishing even her first helping. She was thinking at such a furious rate that her brain was robbing the blood her mouth and stomach needed to appreciate the meal. As soon as she could politely leave the table, she shut herself in her room with the phone and spent a long time talking to Woody. Before the call was over, she was smiling — really smiling — for the first time in days.

The next morning she hung around outside Alice's homeroom until her co-star appeared. "Listen," she said hurriedly, "I've got to talk to you. Meet me in the quad at the start of lunch period. Okay?"

"Sure, but what's — "

"I'll tell you then. I'm late. Lunchtime in the quad, don't forget!" And she rushed off to class.

The morning passed very slowly. Her teachers insisted on breaking into her thoughts with unwanted information about quadratic equations, the NATO alliance, and the proper conjugation of irregular pluperfect verbs. The corridors between classes seemed populated with phantoms. Once she saw a form in the distance that *had* to be Hugh. She went far out of her way to avoid him, only to have him cross her path from a different direction altogether. Another time she saw Michael on his way to orchestra rehearsal with his cello case. She hurried to overtake him, but when she did she discovered that it wasn't Michael at all, but a complete stranger carrying a bass guitar.

Noon found her sitting on her favorite bench in the quad, picking nervously at a loose thread in the seam of her sleeve. She had never thought of herself as the salesman type, but salesmanship was just what the situation demanded. Alice had to hear her out — she had to agree to go along with the scheme Phoebe and Woody had cooked up. Without her, it wouldn't work.

Quarter after. She wasn't coming. Phoebe blamed herself. Of course, Alice didn't want to talk to her after the way Phoebe had been treating her the last few days. Every rehearsal had had its share of little catty remarks, jockeying for Hugh's attention, and not very subtle attempts to make her fellow actress look bad. Alice was dishing it right back at her, it was true, but Phoebe knew that didn't excuse her behavior.

The worst was the way she had acted at the picnic on Sunday. Alice hadn't known any of the people there very well; Phoebe was probably the closest thing she had to a friend. Phoebe should have taken Alice under her wing, introduced her to a few people, and seen to it that she felt at home. Instead she had said a cool hello and ignored her for the rest of the afternoon.

If Alice wasn't going to come to her, she would have to go to Alice. She was gathering her books, getting ready to go in search, when she saw the other girl hurrying across the grass toward her.

"Sorry," Alice said breathlessly, "Miss Perkins kept me after class to talk about my term project. Have you had lunch yet? I'm famished! I was up until two this morning studying my lines, and staying up late always gives me the munchies."

Phoebe quickly revised her plan of talking to her out in the quad. If Alice had food on the brain, she wouldn't be very receptive to a lot of jabber. By now there should be one or two empty tables in the cafeteria, so they could be almost as private as outside. "No, I was waiting for you," she said, unconsciously crossing her fingers. "Let's go."

Once they were through the line and seated, Phoebe moved her tuna sandwich around on its plate and watched Alice tear into a chef's salad with orange-colored dressing. This was going to be harder than she thought.

At the beach, Phoebe belonged to the dive-in-and-get-the-shock-over-with school. The same approach would have to serve her here. "Listen, Alice," she said, leaning across the table and speaking in a low voice, "are you in love with Hugh?"

Alice paused with a forkful of lettuce in midair and stared at her. "Are you?" she demanded in return.

Phoebe held her eyes. "No, I'm not, but he would like me to be. And it's the same thing with you. That's why I asked."

The fork continued to her mouth and Alice began to chew thoughtfully. After a swallow, she said, "Are you trying to get me out of the way so you can have a clear shot at him? Because I'm not going to play."

"If you'd asked me yesterday, and if I'd been honest with you and with myself, I would have said yes." Phoebe couldn't help thinking in acting terms. She was sincere, and she hoped she was projecting that sincerity.

"Now," she continued, "I think I see what's been going on more clearly. I don't want you out of the way at all. I want you to help me straighten out a messed-up situation."

Alice was still wary. She had pushed her salad aside and was listening to Phoebe intently, but

143

she was still keeping her mouth tightly closed.

"Look," Phoebe said into the thickening silence, "somebody's got to take a chance here, and I guess it's me. Hugh told me the other day that he wants to get to know me better — *much* better. The reason he hasn't done anything about it, according to him, is that you have a huge crush on him. He's afraid you might walk out on the show if you see him getting too close to me. I believed him then, but now I don't. Am I right that he said something like that to you, too?"

Alice studied her with narrowed eyes. "Is this some kind of trick?"

"It's no trick. Really."

"All right. Hugh told me you're always trying to get him alone so that you can do a heavy romantic number. He asked me to help him deal with you by sticking around as much as possible. He's afraid that if he rejects you too openly you might mess up the performance."

"That — !"

"*And*," Alice continued, "he hinted that after the show he and I ought to get to know each other better."

"What did you say?"

"That I'd like that. I would, too."

Phoebe frowned. "Hey, you're taking this pretty coolly, aren't you?"

"Am I?"

"You *do* have a crush on him, don't you?"

Alice twirled the straw in her iced tea. "Hugh is a really good director," she said evenly. "He's sensitive, and smart; and he knows a lot about

144

theater and acting. I admire him, and I want to learn what I can from him. I do like him. But I have zero romantic interest in him, if that's what you're asking."

"Oh, come on," Phoebe protested, "I've watched you together!"

"Do you think you're the only one who can act? He works better when he knows he's admired. And like I said, I do admire him. It's not my fault if he's convinced admiration and love are the same thing, is it?"

Phoebe stared at her, then burst out laughing. Talk about wheels within wheels! Hugh was doing his best to manipulate them, and the whole time Alice was manipulating him! "How did we get ourselves into this crazy situation?" she gasped.

"It's the theater," Alice replied. "Everything's more intense there, bigger than life. It has to be, to carry out to the audience, but it's hard to know how to stop when the curtain comes down."

Phoebe sobered instantly. Michael had used almost exactly the same words that night after the prom, trying to explain why Griffin had fallen for his new leading lady, Sarah Carter. For the first time Phoebe felt she understood Griffin, might even someday forgive him.

"You said something about a plan," Alice prompted.

"Yes. I had a long talk with my friend Woody, and he agrees that all these cross-currents are making it impossible to do any real work on the play. They even feel it backstage, on the crew. Not only that, but he gave me some insight as to why Hugh's been behaving like this with you and me. You know how Hugh's studied so much dramatic theory and technique? Well, putting his two female leads at daggers with each other in a production where they play bitter rivals was supposed to make us feel and therefore act our roles more convincingly. The more I thought about it, the more I realized that Woody was right, that had to be Hugh's motive." Alice nodded. Phoebe knew they were together now. "But the technique got out of control and it's backfiring. If we're going to make this play a success, we have to put a stop to the funny business."

"Hm . . . What do we do?"

"Here's my plan. . . ."

That afternoon was to be the first full rehearsal of *Adam and Eve and Helen*. Michael got to the Little Theater as the cast was assembling onstage for Hugh's initial instructions. He left his cello in a safe place and took a seat on the left side of the house, halfway back.

Hugh clapped his hands three times, and the hubbub onstage died out.

"Okay, people," he said, "please pay attention. I want to try running it from the beginning this time. If I have points to make, I'll save them for the end of the act unless there's something hideously wrong. You should all know your lines and entrances by now. But if you don't, or you're not quite sure, carry your script. Don't slow us down by waiting for a prompt. Also, if you're not on in a scene, please come out front. Don't mill around backstage getting in everybody's way.

"All right, then: places for Act One."

After the usual confusion, most of the cast filed down into the audience and the rest disappeared into the wings. The only one left onstage was Alice, playing Eve. Michael glanced down at his copy of the script. He had marked it up crazily with ideas for music, but it was still readable.

> EVE [*looking in her basket*]: Four carrots, half a dozen potatoes, some onions, and a turnip. Is this what they call the fruits of the earth? It won't even make a decent salad. I hate gardening!
>
> [ADAM *enters stage left, looks around puzzled.*]
>
> EVE: Now what? Why does he look at everything but me?
>
> ADAM: Do you remember what I named that tree? I know I named it.
>
> EVE: Which tree?
>
> ADAM: That one, over there, with the orange fruit. That's why I named it, so I wouldn't have to point all the time.

Michael sniffed. The first scene was pretty obvious stuff, but he supposed it would put the audience in a receptive mood for all the philosophy and symbolism to come. He flipped through the script and stopped a few pages later at Helen's entrance. She and Eve had a long dialogue about men, in which Helen defended her approach of letting them come to her, while Eve insisted that women had to use more aggressive tactics. The point being that by the end of the play they would have switched viewpoints entirely.

Michael wondered idly why Phoebe had made such a point of getting him to come to this particular rehearsal. She had really twisted his arm. Maybe it had something to do with the scene between Hugh and her that he had walked in on yesterday. He realized now he should have apologized to her for interrupting them. She had looked very upset when she walked out, and even though he knew it was none of his business, he hoped she knew what she was getting into.

Onstage, Art concluded a speech about the sweat of his brow and exited right. Moments later, Phoebe appeared from behind a curtain upstage center. Michael sat up in his seat. No doubt about it: Phoebe had that mysterious quality called stage presence. Even with a script in her hand, she *was* Helen; or at least she was someone other than Phoebe Hall, someone larger and more imposing.

He noticed that Alice had picked up a script, too. He looked down at his copy. No wonder; this scene contained some of Hugh's longer and more convoluted speeches. Michael let the language wash over him, listening for rhythm rather than sense, trying to decide what sort of melody would create the right transition to the next scene.

Suddenly, something snagged his attention. He listened more carefully. Alice was saying, "It's me he loves, I know it is." Michael didn't recall that in the script.

"And I know he loves *me*," Phoebe countered. "He told me so."

The other actors, seated in the first couple of rows, were exchanging glances. Farther back, behind his improvised desk, Hugh was frozen halfway out of his seat, a script clutched in his hand.

Alice faced Phoebe, hands on hips. "Oh yeah? He told *me* that you're a nasty old thing who has a passion for him! He begged me to protect him from you."

"Is that so?" Phoebe retorted. "Everybody knows you can't keep away from him. The only reason he doesn't tell you where to go is that he's afraid you might leave!"

Michael laughed aloud. That was a pretty good line.

"Ohhh!" Alice started for Phoebe with her hands poised to scratch. "If he didn't think you'd quit, he'd straighten you out right now!"

She attacked, waving her arms like a windmill, but Phoebe put one hand firmly on Alice's head and held her off. Some of the cast chuckled at this classic clown routine.

"Wait a minute," Phoebe said. "Did he really tell you that?"

Alice froze, hands still poised. "Yes. Did he really tell *you* that?"

"Yes."

They both turned their faces to the audience and looked right at Hugh. "He's made monkeys out of us, huh?" Phoebe asked.

"He sure has," Alice agreed, bending her elbows to scratch under her arms like a chimp. There was laughter from backstage.

"Well, how do you think we should teach that big ape a lesson?" Phoebe's voice resounded through the theater.

"Oh, I think he's learning one right now."

Suddenly the Little Theater was echoing with applause as cast and stage crew alike stood to give Phoebe and Alice a spirited ovation. Hugh was on his feet as well, but for a different reason. He straightened his back, turned, and walked up the aisle toward the exit. As he passed, Michael saw that his face had no color in it at all.

The door of the theater swung open, then slammed, and he was gone. The wild clapping continued. After a few moments, though, Phoebe waved for quiet.

"I think Hugh deserved what he just got," she said. Somebody cheered, but she held up a hand. "Maybe next time he thinks about playing games with people's emotions, he'll remember today and think again. But we shouldn't forget why we're here. We're putting on a play, and we're going to give the best performance we can. I don't know if Hugh will come back this afternoon — "

"He'd better not," somebody shouted.

" — but whether he does or not, I think we should rehearse. And when he does come back, we should remember that he *is* the director. He's a pretty good one, too, as long as he sticks to directing. Okay? Okay. Let's get back to work. Places for Act One, Scene Three!"

Chapter
16

Cynthia and Phoebe were sitting on the retaining wall near the flagpole after school on Wednesday. Phoebe had just finished a lively account of the downfall of Hugh Cromwell, as staged by "Eve" and "Helen." Cynthia was doubled over with helpless laugher.

"Talk about turning tables," she said. "Whose idea was it?"

"Yours, in part," Phoebe replied. "That day when we talked in the rain you helped me see that Hugh was leading me on, involving me in some private scheme of his. You weren't the first to say it, but coming from an objective observer it carried a real punch. The actual plot was mine and Woody's, with added details by Alice."

"What happens now, do you think?"

Phoebe laughed. "Now we put on a play! Hugh actually came over to me and Alice at lunch,

151

made a remark about the weather, and left, casually saying that he'd see us at rehearsal!"

"He didn't!"

"He certainly did. It was his way of saying that we were forgiven."

Cynthia was outraged. "Forgiven! *You* weren't the ones who needed to be forgiven!"

"I know, but it doesn't matter. We all know what happened, so what's the use of rubbing his nose in it? The important thing is that he'll be very careful about playing such dangerous games from now on. After all," she added with a grin, "the show must go on!"

"I guess so, but it doesn't seem fair."

"Fairness isn't everything, any more than honesty is. Which reminds me: Have you come clean to your friend about those poems yet?"

"Shh!" Cynthia glanced around. That was as clear an answer to Phoebe's question as any words could have been. "I haven't had a chance yet."

"Well, now you do. Isn't that Bill coming toward us?"

"Where? Oh gosh, you're right! And there *she* is, surrounded by a bunch of her little sophomore friends."

"Now, now," Phoebe said, sliding off the wall and dusting off her jeans, "we were sophomores ourselves not too long ago, don't forget."

"What are you doing? You can't leave now!" Cynthia had to keep herself from clutching at Phoebe's sleeve.

"I've got to. We're rehearsing all afternoon,

breaking an hour for dinner, and going on into the night. That's show biz. Hi."

This last was directed at Bill, who had come over and given each of the girls a despondent nod. Cynthia, seeing that Phoebe was determined to go, said, "Have a good one. I'll fill you in on the latest tomorrow."

"Latest what?" Bill asked as Phoebe strode off toward the Little Theater.

"Hockey scores," Cynthia replied. "Phoebe is a big hockey fan."

"Oh. Doesn't she know that the hockey season ended a month ago?"

"Yes, she does."

"I don't get it." He shook his head. "Not that it matters anyway. I'm glad you're here, Cyn."

She brightened. "You are?"

"Uh-huh. You're the only one who knows what I've been going through the past couple of weeks. I have to communicate with her, and I need you to help me work up my nerve."

Cynthia thought that this request demonstrated enough nerve for any three normal people, but all she said was, "Communicate? What does that mean? Stand on a hilltop waving flags like a Boy Scout? Put an ad in the Personals column of *The Red and the Gold*?"

"Come off it, Cyn. This may seem like a big joke to you, but it isn't to me. It's been a week since I got her last poem, and she still doesn't seem to take the slightest notice of me. At that picnic I stood two feet away from her for ten minutes without getting any reaction at all."

"*Sixteen* minutes," Cynthia said under her breath.

"Um? The point is, I've got to do something more drastic. So I've written her another poem."

Cynthia couldn't help giggling. "That's what I call drastic, all right!"

"I've got it right here, in this envelope," Bill said. "I intend to walk over and hand it to her directly. You don't think that's drastic? She'll have to give me some sign of recognition then."

He stood up from the retaining wall. Cynthia grabbed his shoulder. "Bill, wait!" she cried, trying to gather her scattered wits together. She searched for the right words. Some poet I am, she thought. Where is my eloquence when I need it?

"Bill," she said in a gentler voice, "you don't know this girl at all. You think she's your mysterious poet, but what real evidence do you have? She has the right initials, and you saw her in the hall once when your poet was somewhere nearby. That's really stretching it."

"It doesn't matter, I know inside. I don't understand why she's pretending not to know what lies between us, but I've got to get it straightened out. That's why I'm going to give her this message, in a way that she'll have to respond to. I'm going to *force* her to talk to me!"

You sure will! thought Cynthia.

She had to try again. "If she were the right girl, don't you think she would have given some kind of sign by now? According to what you've told me, your poet is in love with you — "

"She is! And I'm in love with her!"

Cynthia's heart was pounding so loud now that she was sure he would hear. "Does that girl over there look like she's in love with you? She's not paying any attention to you at all!"

"I know, and I don't get it. That's why I have to give her this poem."

"Then go ahead!" Cynthia stamped her foot. She had done her best, but it wasn't good enough. She was furious. "Make a fool of yourself, see if I care!"

Bill looked at her, astounded by the sudden outburst. Then he turned and walked across to where Carol was standing with four or five friends. Cynthia saw Bill hand something to Carol, and she saw Carol read it. She couldn't hear what was said, but she saw as plain as day Carol's look of surprise change to one of amusement while Bill's look of hope turned to embarrassment.

He started back toward Cynthia, walking quickly. When Carol and her friends burst into hysterical giggling, Bill looked at Cynthia and shrugged. She saw the disappointment on his face and her heart went out to him. Suddenly he whirled and started back toward the group of girls. Cynthia clapped her hand to her mouth. This was just too much.

Cynthia watched, flabbergasted, as he stopped in front of Carol, drew himself up to full height, and said in a ringing voice, "I made a mistake.

That was not meant for you. May I please have it back?"

Carol seemed intimidated. Wordlessly she handed the envelope to him. Without a glance at it, Bill thrust it into the back pocket of his jeans, turned on his heel, and walked rapidly away. A hubbub broke out the moment his back was turned, but he paid no attention to it. Cynthia shook her head with admiration. That crazy guy! She hurried after him and caught up to him as he turned down the hill toward the river.

He looked at her and smiled when she slipped her arm through his. "You were right," he said. "I'm a fool. I owe you a pizza for calling this one."

She squeezed his arm. He wasn't ready yet to hear what she had to say, and in any case she was still praying for divine intervention of some sort. Once Bill found out the truth, he was bound to hate her. She wanted to be the friend with the shoulder to cry on for a little longer.

Bill was silent, locked in his thoughts, until they came to the canal. He leaned on the railing, staring down into the water. "I should have listened to you, Cynthia. That's pretty obvious now! But I was so *sure*. I can't even explain it. I looked at that perfectly ordinary girl, that complete stranger, and I convinced myself that I was totally in love with her. And she — she didn't even really exist! I made her up. Am I bonkers or what, Cyn?"

She hesitated. "I think I know what you were feeling," she said in a tentative voice. "You were

156

looking for certain things, certain qualities, and because you wanted so badly to find them, you imagined you saw them in a real person. Everybody does that. That's what love at first sight is all about. And sometimes when we get to know the person better, we're a little disappointed, because they're not exactly the way we thought they were."

Bill reached down, picked up a small rock, and threw it into the canal. The lonely plunk it made pleased him. It sounded exactly the way he felt.

Cynthia tried again. "Bill, everybody makes mistakes."

He snorted.

"Well, really," she insisted, "I've made mistakes, too, and you're lucky that yours doesn't hurt anyone else but yourself. In a couple of days you'll have forgotten all about old C. W."

Her light, affectionate tone brought a smile to Bill's face. Still, when he spoke, his voice trembled. "I'm only asking what I did that was so stupid. All I wanted was to be with someone who understood me, who felt the way I do about things. Someone I could take walks with and look at sunsets, and listen to music, and lie on the beach with. When I read that first poem, I was so sure that I had found her. I wanted so badly for it to be so."

Cynthia's chest tightened until she could scarcely breathe. You did find her! she wanted to shout. She's right here beside you! She turned to Bill to speak, her cheeks pink. But he was still looking down at the water. He hadn't noticed that his poet was shining out of Cynthia's eyes.

"It wasn't just the first poem, either," he continued thoughtfully. "I wrote back, remember, and she answered me. Twice! And each time I was more sure that this was the one. That's why I was so determined to find out who she was, and why I got so crazy over Carol. I didn't even —"

His jaw dropped. He turned suddenly and grabbed her shoulders. "Cynthia!" he exclaimed. "She's still out there somewhere! I *didn't* make her up, not completely. Those poems are real. It was Charlotte Wodehouse I fell in love with, not Carol Winstanley. Carol's a bust, but somewhere there is a C.W. who's the real thing."

Cynthia's ears buzzed and she thought she might faint. This was the moment. This was the opening she needed to say, I'm Charlotte Wodehouse. He would look at her with amazement. Then he would pull her into his arms, and all her dreams would come true. She gazed into his eyes and parted her lips to speak —

And she couldn't do it. Cynthia thought she must be gasping like a guppy in a fishbowl.

Bill was oblivious to her turmoil. "What really bothers me," he continued, "is why she's gone on keeping her identity a secret. She must know me at least slightly, and she says she has feelings for me as strong as I have for her. Why all the mystery? Why is she playing this game with me?"

"Maybe she's afraid," Cynthia said softly. "Maybe her feelings are so tender, so vulnerable, that she thinks they will be hurt if she exposes them to the light. It's lonely to go on dancing in the shadows, but it's safer, too."

"I know. I can't imagine telling anyone but you what *I've* been going through, and I guess she must feel the same as. . . ."

He trailed off into silence. Cynthia blinked and focused on Bill's face. He was staring at her with wide, disbelieving eyes.

"What did you say?"

"I — " Cynthia tried to recall. Then the realization came flooding in. She had spoken honestly, from her heart, and in doing so she had betrayed the truth.

She straightened her shoulders like a prisoner facing a firing squad.

"*You!* It's been you all along!" She nodded miserably. "The initials, of course! I've been an even bigger fool than I thought. I — " Now it was Cynthia's turn to interrupt. She heard herself begin to babble, and the tears in her eyes kept her from seeing the look of joy that had spread across Bill's face.

"I never meant any of this to happen," she said in a rush, the tears in her eyes overflowing onto her cheeks. "I wanted to show you my poems, but I was scared you wouldn't like them. I wanted to tell you that I cared for you but I was scared that you would laugh, or stop being my friend. I was going to tell you I was Charlotte Wodehouse, but then everything got all mixed up, and I knew if you found out instead of loving me you'd hate me and — "

"But I do love you, Cyn."

Cynthia had turned to run away down the tow path when Bill spoke, and at first the meaning of his words didn't register. She was so certain he'd be cursing that she couldn't believe he was laughing.

She stopped in her tracks and looked up at him.

Sure enough, his eyes were twinkling. All the air left Cynthia's lungs and she sat down on the grass with a thump.

Bill sat down beside her and suddenly his arms were around her. "What — ?" she began to say.

"Shut up, C. W., you crazy girl," he said softly. He kissed the tears from her cheeks, and then he kissed her lips. "Save it for a poem."

Coming soon...
Couples #11
MORE THAN FRIENDS

Brenda put her arms around Brad and held him close to her, savoring a moment of togetherness. Just then Ted tapped on Brad's shoulder. "Let's switch Austins," he suggested.

"Sure, I don't mind," Brad said.

Brenda didn't let go of him. "Are you sure?" she whispered in his ear. Ted's timing couldn't have been worse.

"Sure, go ahead. I'll be fine," Brad said.

"Chris and I just thought it was time for a change of pace," Ted said.

Brenda looked at Chris and wondered how much say her stepsister really had in the matter. "So, are you enjoying the party?"

"I am now," he said. A slow Lionel Richie song began to play, and Ted wrapped his muscular arms tightly around Brenda.

"Have you and Chris had a chance to talk tonight?" Brenda asked.

"Not really, But things are okay, I guess. I've

been feeling a lot more relaxed about everything ever since we talked at the sub shop."

"I'm glad, Ted. I've got to admit, it's nice to feel needed. Brad's got his act so completely together that I sometimes wonder, even though I know he cares about me, if he really needs me."

"Well, right now, Brenda, I need you, and you're helping me a lot." Ted was nearly a foot taller than Brenda, and as the conversation ended, he pulled her closer, resting his chin on top of her head. She searched the dance floor for Chris and Brad, but they had left. She saw them at last through the kitchen window, talking, with their backs to the dance floor.

As the music ended, Ted kept one arm around Brenda. With the other, he lifted her chin toward his face. "Thanks, Bren," he said. Then before Brenda even knew what was happening, he leaned down and kissed her softly on the lips.

"Um, you're welcome, Ted," Brenda said when he released her. "I think we should go look for Brad and Chris, don't you?"

"Sure. I think I saw them go toward the house." He looked so relaxed that Brenda was angry at herself for suspecting that his kiss was anything more than friendly gratitude.

CHEERLEADERS™

Join the Team!

They're talented. They're fabulous-looking. They're winners! And they've got what you want! Don't miss any of these exciting CHEERLEADERS books!

Watch for these titles! $2.25 each

- ☐ QI 33402-6 **Trying Out** *Caroline B. Cooney*
- ☐ QI 33403-4 **Getting Even** *Christopher Pike*
- ☐ QI 33404-2 **Rumors** *Caroline B. Cooney*
- ☐ QI 33405-0 **Feuding** *Lisa Norby*
- ☐ QI 33406-9 **All the Way** *Caroline B. Cooney*
- ☐ QI 33407-7 **Splitting** *Jennifer Sarasin*
